FACE THE MUSIC

Dazzlingly talented orchestral violinist Allegra is travelling to Spain for a concert tour when she bumps into the last person on earth she wants to see: her ex-fiancé Zack. But love might just find a way to give their relationship the second chance it so richly deserves! However, there will be plenty of drama — including a stolen violin, secrets from the past, mysterious photos and an unexploded World War Two bomb — before Allegra finds her happy ever after...

FACE THE MUSIC

Dazzlingly talented orchestral violinist Allegra is travelling to Spain for a concert tour when she bumps into the last person on earth she wants to see: her ex-fiancé Zack. But true love might just find a way to give their relationship the second chance it so richly deserved. However, there will be plenty of drama — including a stolen violin, secrets from the past, mysterious photos and an unexploded World War Two bomb — before Allegra finds her happy ever after...

JENNY WORSTALL

◆

FACE
THE
MUSIC

Complete and Unabridged

LINFORD
Leicester

First published in Great Britain in 2021

First Linford Edition
published 2022

*A catalogue record for this book is available
from the British Library.*

ISBN 978–1–4448–4971–4

A Face From the Past

Allegra saw him before he saw her. The width of his shoulders, the dark shiny curls creeping over his collar, that particular way of standing — all unmistakeable.

He turned round.

'Allegra?' he frowned. 'It is you! Allegra, long time no see.'

'Aren't you going to introduce me?'

Allegra looked at the tall blonde beside Zack.

'Of course! Allegra, this is Vanessa; Vanessa, meet Allegra.'

Vanessa smiled, displaying perfectly even teeth.

'Charmed! Come on, Zack, we need to get going. Our flight's already been called. Switzerland awaits!'

'OK, honey.'

Zack picked up his battered leather case; he always took his precious musical scores as hand luggage.

Allegra dug her nails into her hand.

1

With such an early start, she hadn't made any sort of effort with her appearance. She must look a complete frump.

As if Zack would have any interest in how she looked, though.

Still, it had been a whole 12 months — an entire year — since she had last seen Zack and she had to bump into him at Gatwick at seven in the morning, with an extremely pretty girl on his arm.

It wasn't the way she had imagined meeting up again with the love of her life. Not at all.

★ ★ ★

'Orange juice? Certainly, madam. With ice?'

Allegra accepted the drink gratefully and turned to face her friend, Holly, as they sat together in the plane.

'Here's to us,' Holly said as she touched her plastic cup against Allegra's. 'Doesn't quite sound the same as glass, does it?'

Allegra grinned.

'Here's to a great trip to Barcelona. I hear the concert hall's beautiful.'

'Certainly is,' Holly replied. 'Air-conditioned, too, from what I remember. I played there last year, with another orchestra. The hotel was comfortable, as well.'

Allegra settled back in her seat, adjusting it so that she was reclining.

'Did you find what you wanted in duty free?' she asked Holly.

'I had a ball! Made a good start on my Christmas list. I'm surprised you didn't join me.'

'I wanted to get on with reading my Kindle.' Allegra shuffled a little in her seat. 'You'll never guess who I chanced upon, when I was looking for a place to sit down in the waiting area next to the shops.'

'Brad Pitt?'

Allegra shook her head.

'The Tooth Fairy? No? What about Genghis Khan?

'It's no good, you'll have to tell me, Allegra. I'm not a mind reader.'

Allegra bit her lip and stared out of the window at a bunch of fluffy clouds in the shape of a large sofa.

What she wouldn't give to be floating out there, all thoughts of Zack banished from her mind for ever.

'What is it?' Holly put her hand on Allegra's arm. 'Who did you see?'

'You have to guess,' Allegra replied. 'A well-known musician. A conductor.'

'Not that awesome young woman who conducted the first night of the Proms this year?' Holly's eyes sparkled. 'She's amazing — I would have asked for her autograph.'

'No. A man.'

'Not — oh, Allegra, was it . . . ?'

'Yes.'

The tears threatened to flow. Not now, Allegra thought fiercely. I'm not going to let myself cry in public.

Holly's hand moved again to pat Allegra.

'Please don't be upset,' she said. 'It's not worth it. Whatever happened between you is over. You have to forget him, you deserve better.'

'I don't care any more. It was just the shock of seeing him, that's all.' Allegra turned her head to the side. 'I think I'll have a little snooze.

'It's a busy time ahead of us, with rehearsals and two concerts to pack into the next few days, so I need to recharge my batteries.'

It was easy to lie, to say she didn't care any more, but it wasn't true and Allegra knew it.

Her thoughts on waking every morning were of Zack. He occupied her mind and heart every moment of every day, and he was her last thought before sleep.

She had tried to forget him but without success. She'd even been on a few dates with other men, mostly engineered by Holly in an attempt to help her move on, but they'd all come to nothing.

She had met some perfectly pleasant men but they all had one fault in common, a fault she found it impossible to overlook. They weren't Zack.

Zack, however, seemed to be coping

5

fine. Vanesa's perfect face appeared in front of Allegra and she opened her eyes quickly to make it disappear.

Vanessa was about as different from Allegra as it was possible to be. She had the sort of looks models aspire to.

And her hair! How on earth did she get it to be so straight and shiny, especially at that hour of the morning?

'Holly.' Allegra sat up and stretched her legs out as much as was possible in the budget seats.

'I'm here.' Holly put down her magazine. 'Ready and waiting. I knew you'd want to talk.'

Allegra smiled.

'You're a good friend. I promise I won't go on and on about this.'

'You can go on about it as much as you want.'

'No, I mustn't. It's not fair on you and I need to put him out of my mind, I know that.

'It'll probably be easier for me to forget him now.'

Holly drummed her nails on the little

plastic table in front of her.

'You mean because you've seen him again? I thought the opposite would be true — that seeing him again might stir up old memories.'

'No, it'll be easier now,' Allegra insisted. 'Because I saw the ring on her finger. Zack's grandmother's ruby ring; the engagement ring.'

Holly gasped.

'You mean the ring you . . . ?'

'Yes, the ring I threw back in his face a year ago, when we split up.'

Who is Texting?

'Have you heard from Allegra, Pete? Has the plane landed yet?'

Allegra's mother was sitting with her husband in the kitchen of their Bath home.

'Relax,' Pete said. 'She'll contact us when she can. And she is twenty-five, you know! She doesn't have to account for her every move.

'Allegra's grown up, with a proper job, in case you'd forgotten. And she's travelling with Holly, no doubt with lots of other colleagues, too, so what could go wrong?'

Cathy sighed.

'I know you think I worry too much. It's not as if I think anything's going to go wrong, exactly, but I like to know when she arrives after a journey.

'Especially when it's abroad, and especially when she flies.'

Pete put his hand out to Cathy and she clutched it gratefully.

'Most of what you worry about will never happen, you know.'

'But look what did happen!' Cathy began. 'I don't think she's ever totally recovered from all that business with Zack.'

She fiddled with one of her earrings.

'He seemed such a suitable partner for her, with their shared interest in music and so on. They were going to build a life together.'

'He wasn't right for her,' Pete said. 'Not good enough for our Allegra. Truth be told, I never thought it would work.'

'Yes, you did.' Cathy smiled. 'Your memory's playing tricks now, Pete. You said you were proud he was going to be your son-in-law.

'And you kept going on about him, saying how pleased you were that your daughter was going to marry an up-and-coming orchestral conductor.

'Not to mention the countless jokes you used to make when he was here about collecting fares, as if he were a bus conductor!

9

'You were looking forward to having Zack as your son-in-law. The son you never had.'

'That's not how I remember it, not at all.' Pete coughed. 'Not good enough for her,' he repeated obstinately. 'But at least she's over him.'

'Is she?' Cathy asked. 'I've never thought so. She seems different, more subdued somehow. Lost her sparkle.'

'Maybe, but it doesn't do to dwell on it.'

'My dearest wish is that she should meet someone else, someone who'll sweep her off her feet.'

'It'll happen. Give it time.'

'But it's been a year already. Time's ticking on; the biological clock . . .'

'Now you're being silly.' Pete put his arms round his wife. 'Allegra's got a very bright future ahead of her; it'll all work out in the end, you'll see.

'She's bound to meet plenty of new people in that job of hers, rattling round the world as she does. One of them will be right for her.'

'It was easy for us,' Cathy said, 'meeting in our first week at college, then both going on to be teachers in nearby schools.'

'We were lucky,' Pete agreed.

Cathy looked at the photograph of their wedding day which sat proudly on the dresser.

Two faces smiled at her, both a little slimmer and quite a lot younger, but with the same expression of love beaming out of them.

Next to the wedding photo was a picture of Allegra taken when she was ten. With a serious expression on her face, she was playing a solo on her violin. She wore a long frilly blue dress and white shoes.

Her talent and dedication had meant a busy and exciting time for the family as they took her hither and thither for lessons, rehearsal and concerts.

When Allegra had graduated top of her class from the Royal College of Music Cathy and Pete had been overwhelmed with joy and pride.

A sudden beep came from Cathy's phone.

'I bet that's her now,' Pete said.

Hi, Mum and Dad! I've arrived safely with Holly, after an uneventful journey. It's so much hotter here than the UK — glad I brought lighter clothes.

Our hotel room is lovely and nearly as big as our whole flat in London!

Got to dash — rehearsal shortly. Another rehearsal and concert tomorrow.

A x

PS Holly sends her best wishes.

'What did I tell you?' Pete said, reading over Cathy's shoulder. 'Now, I'd better be off — need to be at the golf club in half an hour.'

'I can't think why you're bothering,' Cathy said. 'You said you hated golf, couldn't understand why grown men would chase a tiny ball around a vast stretch of grass with a metal stick all day for no good reason.'

Pete raised an eyebrow.

'I said that?'

'Yes, you did!'

'Nevertheless, I thought I'd give it a go.

I've been offered another guest pass for the day so I might as well use it.'

'Have a good time,' Cathy called to Pete as he left. 'Hope it doesn't rain!'

Cathy reckoned Pete must be finding his retirement more tedious than he was letting on, if he was prepared to try golf again.

A quick glance at her watch told her she, too, should be moving.

She had also recently retired, but whereas Pete was casting around somewhat forlornly for activities to occupy his time, her timetable seemed to have filled up all on its own, to bursting point.

Cathy picked up her bag and took her jacket from the back of the chair. She was all set to go.

Hang on, nearly forgot my phone, she thought. That would have been a disaster.

★ ★ ★

13

She soon arrived at St Mildred's Charity Shop where she was due to cover a shift for a sick friend.

'Hello! Tea?' Maeve, one of Cathy's closest friends, rushed towards her, arms full with a jumble of garments and three pairs of shoes balanced precariously on the top.

'Have we got time?' Cathy asked. 'There seems so much to do.'

'Of course we've got time!' Maeve roared with laughter. 'Life isn't worth living if you haven't time for tea.

'Now, be a dear and stick the kettle on.'

Cathy did as she was told and soon the two friends were sorting and chatting while sipping Earl Grey.

'Look at this,' Maeve said, holding a tattered, purple-sequined, net micro-skirt across her ample hips. 'Think it would suit me?'

'How can I put this tactfully,' Cathy began. 'Actually I can't, so, no! It doesn't suit you — any more than this thing suits me.'

She flung a full-length, bright pink, fake-fur stole across her shoulder and rolled her eyes suggestively.

Maeve hooted and plonked an Austrian-style hat complete with feather on to Cathy's head.

'Maybe with this? Or this, perhaps,' she suggested, adding a shredded silk scarf in vibrant colours.

'Hang on!' Cathy wheezed. 'You've got to stop making me laugh.'

'Why?' Maeve demanded.

'Because my phone beeped,' Cathy said. 'I must have a text. I'd better check it in case anything's wrong.'

She picked up her phone, then frowned.

'Wait a minute,' she said. 'This is Pete's phone. Mine's in my bag as well.

'He must have left his on the table and I brought them both out with me by mistake.'

'Never mind.' Maeve started tidying up the mess they'd created. 'The man can do without his phone for a day, can't he?'

'I'm sure he can, but that's not what concerns me.'

Cathy squinted at the small screen, not quite able to believe her eyes.

Maeve priced the Austrian hat at £2.50 and arranged it on a nearby shelf.

'What exactly is concerning you?'

Cathy held Pete's phone up to show to Maeve.

'Who is Alice?' she asked. 'And why is she leaving a message to my husband saying, 'See you soon'?'

In Barcelona

The sound of excited chatter and instruments of all shapes and sizes being put through their paces was deafening as Allegra pushed open the door with her back, carefully cradling her violin and bow.

'Not too late!' Holly gave a sigh of relief. 'I thought the taxi driver would never get us here in time.'

After a delayed landing, the two friends had made their way from Barcelona airport to their hotel, dumped their bags, and rushed to the concert hall in the city centre for the first rehearsal.

They slipped across the stage to the back of the first violins and sat down hastily.

'Look! There's the flautist I met in Rome last week.' Allegra waved cheerfully to a petite woman in a purple dress.

'And over there — isn't he the double-bass player from Dubai?' Holly grinned. 'I was hoping I'd see him again.'

'Quiet, ladies and gentlemen, please.'

The orchestra manager looked round at the musicians until he had their full attention, before continuing in the deepest bass voice with a hint of a soft welsh lilt.

'May I welcome Maestro Rostopovsky?'

The orchestra cheered as a diminutive figure clad in black walked to the podium.

'Good afternoon.' He took a small bow and clutched his hand to his heart.

'I'm delighted to be here and cannot wait for our concert tomorrow. My beloved Beethoven — what could be better?'

Maestro Rostopovsky coughed, then raised his baton in a gnarled claw-like hand.

'Let's play!'

The orchestra leaped into action and the familiar opening of Beethoven's 'Symphony No. 5' filled the auditorium.

Allegra relaxed into the piece. She would never tire of listening to Beethoven. Each time she was asked to play this gem it seemed as fresh to her ears as the first time she'd heard it, aged seven, listening to a concert on the radio with her father.

She had sat quite still, in a trance, as she'd listened. Pete, amazed at her reaction, had started taking her regularly to classical concerts in Bristol after that.

Maestro Rostopovsky wiped his face with a large handkerchief during a pause in the music.

'He looks a bit tired,' Holly whispered to Allegra.

'He's pulling at his collar,' she replied. 'He doesn't look terribly comfortable, does he?'

'It is rather airless in here,' Holly said. 'So much hotter than England.

'Oh, here we go. Starting again . . .'

★ ★ ★

During the mid-rehearsal break Holly and Allegra took the chance to nip outside and get some fresh air. Quite a few of the players were already outside, drinking glasses of water and exchanging gossip.

'How much did you pay for a set of strings?'

'I can't tell you, but let's just say it was eye-watering.'

'So, after that fiasco, were you asked to play in the next concert?'

'Sadly not!'

'And did the percussion player ever say sorry?'

'No, but he will.'

'How did you manage, when you found you'd forgotten your concert clothes?'

'Luckily we weren't far from a certain well-known chain store. I had time to nip in and buy a black top and skirt and I managed to borrow a pair of black shoes from one of the ladies in the box office.'

'It's going to be a great concert,' Holly said. 'And it's so much fun out here, listening to everyone.'

'Absolutely!' Allegra gave a wide grin.

'I'm surprised by how many of this bunch I've worked with before. It's our musical family!'

'There seems to be a lot more arriving now,' Holly commented.

'Yes, they must be the choir,' Allegra said. 'They're in the second piece in the concert.'

'Mozart?'

'Yes. 'Mass In C'. I've performed it a few times. You?'

'Yes, I played it a couple of years ago in Vienna,' Holly answered.

'That must be one of the solo singers,' Allegra said as a tall blond creature swept past them, a coat artfully draped over one shoulder to display its red silk lining.

'He looks like a Greek god!' Holly said, completely enraptured by the vision.

'He does, rather,' Allegra agreed. 'He'll set hearts fluttering in the choir, no doubt about it.'

'Maybe the orchestra, too,' Holly murmured as they made their way back to the rehearsal.

Half an hour later the concert hall was filled with pulsating music as the soloists, choir and orchestra all poured their hearts into Mozart's breathtaking melodies.

Then disaster struck.

Clutching at his chest, Maestro Rostopovsky called for some water and looked as if he were about to collapse.

The Greek-god singer rushed to his aid and in the nick of time caught the frail conductor before he hit the floor.

'Aah!' the chorus cooed.

'What a hero!' the bass player from Dubai asserted.

'Right place, right time,' the flautist in purple said.

'Can we have some help here?' the Greek god shouted. 'Is there a doctor here? Maybe one of the choir?'

'I'm a doctor!' one of the altos called as she jumped down from the choir steps and rushed to help. 'Here, let me. Thank you for catching him, you've done a grand job. What is your name?'

'Boris. Boris the bass. At your service.'

'Aah!' the choir cooed again. 'Boris the bass.'

'Maybe if everyone were to sit down?'

Boris suggested. 'Quiet, please. Let the doctor assess the patient.'

After a tense few minutes, it was decided the maestro had been overcome by overwork, heat and dehydration. As a precaution, he had better be taken to hospital to be checked over.

'Is there a conductor in the choir?' Boris asked. 'Or in the orchestra? Someone who could conduct the rest of the rehearsal?

'No? Then I will offer myself to help our musical forces in their hour of need.'

Without further ado, he leaped on to the podium, raised his hands high above his head and yelled.

'Let's start from the next chorus, ladies and gentlemen! Look my way, breathe . . .'

'He's not bad,' Holly whispered to Allegra.

'No, indeed,' she answered. 'I wouldn't like to have to conduct this lot at short notice, would you? He has courage.'

At that precise moment, Boris turned to look at Allegra. He fixed her with a beaming smile followed by a cheeky wink.

She felt hot and cold all over, lingering thoughts of Zack firmly squeezed out of her mind.

★ ★ ★

Later, back at the hotel in the room they were sharing, Holly and Allegra collapsed on to their beds, worn out by all the drama.

'It's been a long day,' Holly said.

'Too right! Delayed flight, extra-long rehearsal . . .'

'I hope the maestro will be all right for tomorrow.'

'He should be fine,' Allegra said. 'He probably needs a rest and then he can take over again in the morning.'

'Maybe not,' Holly said, looking at her phone.

'What do you mean?'

'There's an e-mail from the orchestral manager,' Holly explained. 'They've decided Maestro Rostopovsky shouldn't do the concert but must rest and restore himself.'

'Is Boris going to conduct?'

'Sadly not. He's needed as the bass soloist. They say they've been lucky to be able to get someone well-known who's agreed to fly over immediately from Switzerland.'

'No! Not . . . ?' Allegra sat upright on her bed, her eyes wide with shock.

'Yes. Sorry, Allegra. It's Zack. He's flying here overnight from Zurich so as to be here as soon as possible.

A New Interest

'Who is Alice, Pete? Tell me.'

Cathy stared at herself in the long mirror in her bedroom, practising what she would say to her husband when she next saw him.

This had been Maeve's advice after Cathy had shared her discovery of Pete's unusual text from the mysterious Alice.

'You need to rehearse asking him who this Alice is. Make sure your expression is non-threatening, because it's all a huge mistake, you know that.

'But you need to be clear and you have the right to know what's going on,' Maeve had said.

Cathy had closed her eyes for a brief moment on hearing this. The situation seemed completely unreal to her.

What did Maeve suspect Pete of doing? Surely she couldn't be suggesting Pete would be carrying on with someone.

Her Pete? The very idea was laughable. They'd been married for the best part of her adult life. Yet it was a strange message to find.

'No,' Cathy muttered to herself. 'I'm not questioning Pete like this. It's ridiculous! I trust him implicitly.

'The poor man must have got himself into some sort of situation or muddle, that'll be what's going on. The best thing is if I simply ask him.

'Hello, love! I'm home. Fancy a cuppa?' Pete's voice floated up the stairs.

Cathy pulled herself together.

'Be down in a second!' she called. 'And, yes, tea would be lovely.'

Soon the pair of them were sitting outside relaxing in the autumn sunshine.

'Had a good time?' Cathy asked.

'Yes,' Pete replied. 'I popped into the library to change my books and went to the information session about all the new adult education courses, too.'

'You said there was going to be a talk in the library when you were browsing on the computer a few days ago. Does anything sound interesting?'

'Cooking,' Pete replied. 'I thought,

you've been soldiering on in the kitchen all these years and I'd like to give you a break and have a go myself. What do you think?'

'I think it's a great idea,' Cathy said. 'When do you start?'

'Alice says I can start tomorrow.'

'Alice?'

'She was giving the talk,' Pete explained. 'She's in charge of bookings for the courses. I messaged her a few days ago through the council website and she's been encouraging me to find out more about the sort of course I'd like to do.'

'Fantastic!' Cathy jumped up and gave Pete a hug. 'You have no idea how happy I am.'

'What's going on?' Pete asked. 'You're behaving oddly.'

Cathy hung her head.

'You know me too well.'

Pete scratched his ear.

'Cathy, what is it?'

Cathy cleared her throat.

'I found a message from Alice on your

phone yesterday, when I took your phone by accident. I didn't know what to think, to be honest.'

'Cathy!' Pete roared with laughter. 'You know you're the only woman in the world for me. For ever.'

'I know,' Cathy murmured as Pete gathered her into a bear-like hug. 'It's so silly. I shouldn't even have looked at your phone, but I thought it was mine, and then Maeve said . . .'

'I might have known Maeve would be involved,' Pete said. 'I feel sorry for her, with her over-active imagination.

'The woman watches so many melodramatic soaps and films, she sees intrigue everywhere and views everyone with suspicion, all with no good reason.'

'Dear Maeve,' Cathy protested. 'Everyday life must seem tame to her after all those years running the school as headmistress. She used to rule the place with an iron grip — though with a very tender heart, too.'

'Yes, I suppose she must miss all that, the everyday conflicts and situations she was so good at dealing with. I bet she runs the charity shop efficiently.'

'She certainly does. There was a moth there last week, and within minutes Maeve had tracked down the bag of clothes it had had the temerity to fly out of.

'She then traced the donor of the bag, rang her up and gave her quite an earful of advice down the phone.'

'Advice or abuse?' Pete sniggered.

'Advice! Behave yourself, Pete.'

'What happened to the moth?' Pete asked. 'No, don't tell me. You know how much I hate blood sports.'

'In that case, let's just say it came to a sticky, but mercifully quick end.

'But seriously, it's true Maeve has always been keen to share her views.'

'Don't I know it!' Pete said thoughtfully. 'She used to give us plenty of parenting advice when Allegra was small.'

'Indeed she did,' Cathy said, 'although I have to admit some of it was very useful.

She always meant well.'

Cathy sighed.

'Allegra told me that Maeve even tried to advise her about Zack once they were engaged.'

'But Maeve wouldn't know anything about that,' Pete argued, 'not being married or attached to anyone.'

'Maybe that's why she felt no compunction about offering advice so freely,' Cathy replied.

'What? Oh, I see what you mean. She wasn't held back by any sort of reference to reality or experience.' Pete nodded.

'Exactly! Her romantic experiences have been exclusively informed by television and those novels she's always getting out of the library with the lurid covers.'

'Those ones with a dagger and a heart on the front, perhaps with a pool of blood in the corner?' Pete suggested. 'I used to confiscate those when I was teaching if I saw them sticking out of a sixth-former's bag.'

'You book snob!'

'I gave them back at the end of the day,'

Pete reassured Cathy. 'Mainly because I didn't want them in my possession any longer than strictly necessary!'

'We get quite a lot of that sort of reading matter in the charity shop,' Cathy mused. 'Maeve always puts the books on a high shelf.'

'So only she can reach them?' Pete sniggered again.

'Poor Maeve,' Cathy said. 'I feel sorry for her now. She must be at a bit of a loose end sometimes, with no close family. I wish I could do something to help.'

'You do help her, by volunteering at the charity shop. You even fill in when other people are absent.'

'Yes, it was a bit beyond the call of duty yesterday — but we had a lot of fun.' Cathy smiled at her husband.

'In between suspecting me of goodness knows what?'

'Point taken. Actually, Pete, I didn't suspect you of anything untoward — of course I didn't. I was concerned, though, because I thought you might have got yourself in a muddle again.

'You remember when you first stopped work and started sorting everything out in the house?

'Rearranging all my belongings, putting my herbs and spice jars in alphabetical order, books in order of size, all neatly lined up in such a way I was scared to disturb the display by taking one out of the bookcase to read!'

'Guilty as charged,' Pete agreed.

'And then you started chucking stuff away. Including some things we needed!'

'Yes, that was hard work,' Pete said, wiping his hand across his brow. 'I feel tired just thinking about how I went up and down the ladder to the loft umpteen times a day.'

'Luckily I managed to sneak a few prize pieces back,' Cathy said. 'And what about the shed? Remember clearing the shed?'

'I certainly do! We found some real treasures.' Pete smiled. 'The hoard of rusty nails, rolls of garden twine turning to green dust, the massive collection of plastic plant pots, impossible to recycle.'

'All destined for the dump. And after you'd got rid of that rubbish, you started buying up tons of items we didn't need on eBay.'

Pete hung his head in mock shame.

'Sorry.'

'No need to apologise. It was another step on your journey towards accepting retirement. So I thought, maybe . . .'

'I see,' Pete said. 'You thought perhaps I was behaving in a, how can I put it? Slightly eccentric way again.'

'The next phase along my journey of trying to find out what to do with the rest of my life?'

'That's it,' Cathy said. 'I thought Alice could have been part of your next harebrained scheme. Maybe an acupuncturist, or a hang-gliding instructor, or a teacher from a fitness boot camp!'

'Steady on!' Pete laughed and swept Cathy into his arms. 'So you approve of the cookery classes?'

'Definitely,' Cathy replied. 'I'll give you a list of my favourite dishes.'

'No need,' Pete said. 'I know them all

already and I used a spreadsheet on my phone to plan some menus while I was on the bus coming home.

'I'm going to start by learning to make a quiche.'

'That's ambitious for someone who's not, well, au fait with the kitchen.'

'Why do you think I'm going on the course?'

Pete's logic was impeccable and Cathy was pleased to see her husband looking enthusiastic.

She'd been worried for some time that he wasn't enjoying his retirement as much as he should.

And he had been through some rather annoying phases — who could forget the time he decided to get up at 5.30 every morning to write his memoirs?

Thank goodness that hadn't lasted too long — it couldn't, as he'd become totally exhausted and had succumbed to man 'flu.

'You'll have a great time at your new course,' Cathy said. 'Maybe I should look out a pinny for you?'

'I don't think men wear pinnies in the kitchen,' Pete said. 'I thought I'd take my old boiler suit with me; it'll be just the ticket.'

'It's covered in oil!' Cathy protested, 'And it will be far too hot. I've got a better idea. I saw a chef's apron in the charity shop yesterday — I'll give Maeve a quick ring and see if it's still there.'

'OK,' Pete said. 'I'm going to have a look at my spreadsheet again. The course starts on Thursday and I want to be ready.'

As Cathy was about to call Maeve, she saw a text on her phone from Allegra.

Hi Mum!
Our conductor's ill and Boris the bass, one of the soloists, has taken over rehearsals until the substitute arrives.
The new conductor is Zack, he's arriving soon.

Stolen!

'Hello, everyone!' Zack strode on to the platform where the orchestra and choir were assembled. 'It's terrific to be here.'

He shook Boris's hand.

'Thanks for keeping the show on the road — I've heard you've done a great job. Now, we must get on. From the top, everyone!'

He looked tired, Allegra thought. Black circles under his eyes. He'd lost weight, too, since they were together.

Allegra lifted her bow and allowed herself to forget everything, revelling in Mozart's glorious harmonies.

'Thank you all,' Zack said at the end of the piece. 'I can see Boris has done a fine job keeping it all together.'

Boris grinned and took a bow.

'Now, maybe the singers could all leave quietly? I'll see you tonight at the concert.

'Meanwhile, orchestra, let's go straight into the Beethoven. We've got time for a quick run-through before you all take a well-deserved break.'

Allegra found it harder to concentrate in the Beethoven. As the dramatic chords rang out, she thought back to when everything had started to go wrong for her and Zack.

It had been shortly after they'd become engaged that Allegra had begun to wonder if she'd made the right decision. Zack had seemed to change, to become quieter, almost moody when he should have been happy with so much to look forward to.

Allegra couldn't understand it. Maybe they got engaged too soon — perhaps they hadn't known each other well enough.

It had been a whirlwind courtship with both of them away so often, travelling with different orchestras, sometimes only meeting up for the briefest of times.

Zack had asked her to turn down some work which would have meant travelling to the Far East for a few weeks. He had a big concert coming up in New York and wanted her to be there to support him.

Allegra had said no. She couldn't afford to turn the opportunity down — her career was important to her. Surely he understood?

He'd accused her of not supporting him and they'd had their first real row.

The pair had made up almost immediately, both shocked by the harsh words they'd said to each other and both resolving not to let such a thing happen again.

They decided they should discuss how they would manage their careers, which involving so much touring. After all, once they were married it would be crazy if they were hardly ever in the same country.

Zack pointed out that, as an up-and-coming conductor, he could recommend Allegra for work with whichever orchestra he was invited to conduct.

She wasn't happy with this idea. It would be convenient and help them spend more time together, for sure, but Allegra wanted to be offered jobs on merit, not merely through Zack.

'I haven't worked hard all these years just to give it up and trail after a man,' she argued, surprising herself with the strength of her feelings.

'I'm not just 'a man',' Zack flashed back. 'I'm the person you say you want to spend the rest of your life with — at least that's what you lead me to believe!'

'Of course I do,' Allegra replied. 'Please don't doubt me, Zack. I've always dreamt of a musical career; I'd like to try to sort out what form it'll take after we're married.'

Zak's answer was brief.

'It's hard enough trying to cope with everything — please don't make it harder.'

Allegra wondered what he meant by this comment, but the moment passed before she could ask him to clarify what it was he was struggling to cope with.

He seemed to be hinting at some sort of pre-existing burden but, for the life of her, she couldn't think what it might be.

On another occasion, Zack said that once they were married, and if they were lucky enough to have a family, he wanted Allegra to give up her playing career.

She was shocked to hear this — they hadn't discussed what they would do if and when children arrived.

It might be that she would indeed retire from playing, at least for a number of years. But she wanted this to be something they discussed together, not something to be assumed or, even worse, imposed on her.

These incidents were enough to give the couple a warning to pause before they tied the knot. But in the end, it wasn't disagreeing about the details of their future lives together that drove them apart. It was something else entirely.

★ ★ ★

Allegra was shaken out of her reverie by the fierce ending of Beethoven's 'Symphony No. 5'.

'Magnificent!' Zack said. 'I don't think you lot need a conductor at all. You're incredible! See you all this evening, seven o'clock sharp, backstage.'

'You OK?' Holly asked Allegra. 'I didn't feel you were really with me during the play-through.'

'I'm saving myself for this evening,' Allegra replied. 'Hey, look, isn't that Boris over there?'

'So it is,' Holly said. 'The singers didn't have to stay to hear the Beethoven — I wonder why he did.'

'Hello, ladies,' Boris said as he bounded up to Holly and Allegra. 'I'm collecting people to go out for a bite to eat before the performance. Care to join us?'

'What a great idea!' Holly said. 'How nice of you to ask.'

'Yes, thank you,' Allegra agreed. 'Lovely. We need to leave our violins in the dressing-room — shall we meet you outside in a few minutes?'

'I wouldn't leave anything valuable backstage,' Boris advised. 'Take your instruments with you.'

'You're right; one can't be too careful,' Holly agreed.

'Goodness, I would be heartbroken if

anything happened to my violin,' Allegra added. 'My poor parents practically had to take out a second mortgage to buy this for me when I was at college.'

Allegra glanced over her shoulder to see if she could see Zack, but there was no sign of him.

'He left immediately,' Holly whispered. 'Stop thinking about him.'

'I wasn't,' Allegra replied. 'Just checking, because I don't want to run into him again by accident. I couldn't face it.

'Why would I ever want to see him again?'

'No reason.' Holly rolled her eyes. 'Come on. I'm starving.'

Boris led Holly, Allegra and quite a few others from the orchestra to a popular and crowded restaurant nearby, where they found a bunch from the choir already feasting on local delicacies at an enormously long, wide table near the main doors.

'The restaurant management know we have to eat quickly because of the concert,' Boris explained, 'so I've taken the liberty of ordering tapas.

'There's bound to be something you like; please, sit down and dig in.'

There was quite a party atmosphere and Boris was definitely at the centre of it.

As usual, with any group of musicians, viola jokes were shared freely, particularly by the viola players themselves.

'Oy, Boris! How do you get two viola players to play in tune with each other?'

'That's an old one!' Boris shouted down the table. 'Ask one of them to leave, obviously.'

'What about this one — why do you think viola players don't play hide and seek?'

'I don't know,' Holly said. 'Why don't viola players play hide and seek?'

'Oh, I know this,' Allegra said with a smile. 'Because no-one would look for them.'

'Excellent!' Boris cackled. 'And now the last one, as we need to leave soon to go and get changed for the concert.

'How do you keep a violin from being

stolen? Anybody? No? Put it in a viola case! Get it? Hey, what's the matter, Allegra?'

'My violin! It was here, beside me. Where's it gone? It must have been stolen!'

'Hilarious!' Boris hooted. 'You nearly had me there . . . Hang on, you're not joking, are you? Sweetie, please don't cry. Here, take my handkerchief.'

'I can't have lost it!' Allegra sobbed. 'It means everything to me.

'Oh, please, would you all mind looking around? Maybe it's been moved? Can anyone see it?'

Boris called one of the staff over.

'May we have some help here? Call the police, or something? Look at the CCTV, if you have any.'

'Of course, señor, so sorry. I'm sure we can have this cleared up in a moment.'

The restaurant manager rushed over to the table and tried his best to help, calling the police once it became obvious the violin had well and truly vanished.

'What will you play with this evening

if your violin doesn't turn up in time?' Holly asked.

'No idea,' Allegra said, 'and I can't see it turning up within the next thirty minutes, so I've a real problem.'

'Don't worry,' Boris reassured her. 'I have my violin with me, back in my hotel room. You can borrow it for as long as you need to.'

'You're a singer!' Holly said, astounded.

'I play the violin, too,' Boris replied. 'Badly, I admit, but I always take it on tour and practise when I can.'

Allegra was amazed.

'I know you're thinking of all the jokes about singers,' Boris said. 'How singers have nothing but resonance between their ears. But I promise you I have quite a decent violin in my hotel room and I'm going to rush away and get it.

'It's the least I can do, after encouraging you to bring your violin to the restaurant.'

Before she could help herself Allegra leaned forward and gave Boris a peck on the cheek out of gratitude, at the very moment that Zack walked into the restaurant accompanied by two policemen.

'I heard what's happened,' he said, 'and thought I'd better come and see if I could help.'

Allegra blushed scarlet as she realised Zack must have seen her kiss Boris.

But why should that matter? It wasn't as if Zack had any interest in her.

Besides, I can do what I like, she thought. He's with Vanessa now, his fiancée, and I don't care at all. Couldn't be less interested in the man.

'May we ask you a few questions, madam,' one of the policemen said to Allegra, 'to help with our enquiries?'

'Of course.'

'Are there any identifying marks on the violin or the bow? Anything else in the case to help us identify the stolen property?'

'I've pictures of the violin on my phone,' Allegra said, 'showing the various markings.

'There are a lot of distinguishing features because it's an old, well-used instrument — the same goes for the bow.

'As for the case, I've got the usual spare strings and rosin in there. My initials are engraved on the handle, will that help?'

She sighed.

'Oh, and I had a spare bow in there, too. Nothing fancy, but I always carry a spare.'

Her heart beat faster as she decided not to mention the photographs she had tucked safely down the side of the velvet lining.

She couldn't mention them, not with Zack standing there — her beautiful Zack, lost to her for ever.

How could she say that the photos she carried with her everywhere in the world, and looked at on countless occasions — kissed even — were two tiny, dog-eared snaps from a photo booth of her and Zack, taken on a daytrip to the seaside?

She could see the photos now, imprinted in her mind and heart for ever, the two of them happy and carefree.

Zack's hand was resting lightly on her

shoulder. Both of them were smiling at each other, so much in love.

The photos meant more to her than anything in the world, showing a time when they had had their whole future ahead of them.

Before she'd ruined it.

Culinary Confusion

'This sure has been an eventful trip for Allegra,' Pete remarked a few days later. 'At least the first concert went smoothly, after all the trouble.'

'Yes, but poor Allegra, she's still frantically worried about her violin,' Cathy said. 'The Spanish police don't seem to have made much headway with finding it yet and it'll be more difficult for her to find out how the police are doing once she's back in London.'

'She'll be back by tonight, won't she?' Pete asked.

'Yes. I'm not quite sure what time.'

'Don't worry, love,' Pete said. 'I'm certain the police are doing their best and Allegra can borrow the violin from this Boris chap as long as need be, apparently.'

'I know.' Cathy sighed. 'And her violin is insured, but that's not the point. The instrument means so much to Allegra — she's played on it since she was at college.

'Do you remember when she played 'The Lark Ascending' for the first time?'

Cathy felt her eyes misting over as the vision of her teenage daughter, conjuring a beautiful melody out of her violin and swaying in time to the music, popped into her mind.

'The performance was a triumph,' Pete agreed, 'but there's not much we can do right now except trust the Spanish police and their investigation.'

'It's a shame there wasn't CCTV,' Cathy commented.

'They don't have CCTV everywhere.' Pete smirked. 'Maybe it's not only Maeve who watches too many television dramas!'

Cathy nodded.

'We'll have to wait and trust the police, as you say.'

She grabbed a tea towel and started to clear the draining board.

'This Boris sounds a pleasant sort of guy.'

'Cathy! No matchmaking. It's none of

51

our business.'

'I'm not matchmaking — simply making an observation. He must think something of Allegra if he's prepared to lend her his violin.'

'True and, to be fair, she did say she admired his conducting and the way he took charge when Rostopovsky took ill.'

Pete took a large ceramic dish out of the kitchen cupboard and inspected it carefully.

'Yes, indeed. Wasn't it great Rostopovsky was able to come to the concert, to sit in the audience?' Cathy said. 'Pete, what are you doing?'

'My homework,' Pete said as he opened the fridge door and pulled out some cheese and bacon.

'Oh, how could I forget?' Cathy smiled. 'It's quiche day, isn't it? I'm glad you're enjoying your cookery course.'

'I had a great time at the first class yesterday. The new apron went down a treat. Our tutor said I looked very professional.

'I'm glad you persuaded me not to

wear my old boiler suit — it would have looked a little out of place.'

'Well, I'm glad you followed my advice.' Cathy chuckled and leaned over to kiss him gently on the cheek. 'I'll be off now. I need to pop in to see Mrs Oatcake.'

'Mrs Oatcake? Great name! Who's that?'

'She's one of the ladies I visit when I take library books round — didn't I mention her before?'

Pete looked blank.

'I can't keep up with your good deeds,' he protested. 'I have a vague memory you were considering joining the volunteer library home reading scheme, but I wasn't sure what it involved and I certainly didn't know you'd started.'

'I joined the scheme a while ago,' Cathy said. 'I've visited Mrs Oatcake a few times now — she's not been at all well and requested home library visits.'

'How's it going?'

Cathy cleared her throat before replying.

'I'm sure I'll manage to find some books she enjoys, given time.'

'That well?' Pete hacked some bacon into rough stringy pieces. 'What are you doing after you've visited her?'

'Church flowers, followed by a hair appointment.'

'Oh, yes, you're trying the new place on the high street, aren't you?'

Pete picked up a bit of bacon from the floor and added it to the pile of ingredients for the quiche filling.

'I am.'

'What was it called again?'

'You know perfectly well what it's called.'

'Humour me.'

''Jane Hair'. It's not that funny, Pete!'

'Yes, it is. Is it a trim you're having, or are you perhaps having some Wuthering Highlights?'

Pete wiped tears from his eyes.

'OK,' Cathy said. 'Wuthering Highlights is quite funny.'

'Plenty more where that came from. It reminds me of when I used to sit in the staff room at break with my colleagues, all of us making up the most terrible puns, mostly about the set works we were teaching the kids. I remember —'

'Enough,' Cathy said. 'I'm not in the mood. I'm still worried about Allegra.'

'In what way?'

'I'm concerned she hasn't said anything about Zack.'

'That's good, isn't it?' Pete grated some cheese vigorously, holding his fingers perilously close to the sharp metal spikes.

'Not necessarily. I know her. If she didn't mind seeing him again and working with him, I think she'd have said. It's the silence I find suspicious.

'I do hope she's not been upset by seeing him again.'

'You're worried because she hasn't said she's upset? Ouch, my fingers! Surely if she was upset, she would have told you?' Pete frowned as he started to cut an onion into large irregular chunks.

'It's a feeling I've got. I can't explain.'

Her husband shook his head and carried on chopping.

'I'm worried, but not about Allegra. I'm worried by the amount of chores you're doing for other people,' he remarked.

'I like to keep busy!'

'Mmm. I suppose, as long as you're enjoying it, there's no harm. And now I've got my cookery course, I'm incredibly busy again. I haven't got time to miss my teaching at all!'

'You loved teaching, we both did, but there comes a time . . .' Cathy's voice tailed off into an uncertain silence.

What sort of time was she having now, she wondered.

Maybe she was remembering her work with the rosy tinted glow of hindsight, but nowadays she seemed to be even more at everyone's beck and call than she'd been when in charge of her Reception Class.

What's more, she was finding that some of the characters she had to deal with in her retirement were less well-behaved and mature than some of the little people she'd been in charge of at school.

'Crumbs!' she said, glancing up at the kitchen clock. 'I'd better get my skates on. See you later. I'm already looking forward to the quiche!'

'It's not difficult, this cooking lark, is it, once you get going? I've already made the filling, well, most of it. Pastry next.'

Pete patted the bag of flour in front of him on the table.

'Should those eggs be in the filling?' Cathy pointed at three eggs still in their shells, rolling around precariously on the counter.

'Ah, yes. Thank you. Wouldn't have tasted the same without those little beauties!'

Cathy laughed.

'See you later.'

★ ★ ★

On her way to Mrs Oatcake, Cathy heard her phone ring.

'I hope she's not cancelling,' she muttered, diving into her handbag. 'Oh, it's you, Pete!'

'I'm worried,' Pete said. 'Very worried. I don't think pastry is easy to make. No, not at all. It's so sticky and grey!

'It doesn't look right.'

'Don't worry,' Cathy soothed. 'See if you can roll it out.'

'Roll it out?'

'With the rolling pin?'

'Oh, yes. The tutor said something about a rolling pin. Do we have one?'

'Bottom of the cupboard in the dresser, right-hand side. Got to go, Pete. I'm nearly at Mrs Oatcake's.'

'Thanks, love. I appreciate your help.'

No sooner was Cathy comfortably seated in an armchair in Mrs Oatcake's sitting-room, sipping tea, than her phone went off again.

'Not important,' she said after a hasty glance at the screen. 'My husband. Now, where were we?'

'I was explaining to you what sort of books I thought I would enjoy,' Mrs Oatcake said, 'before your husband interrupted us.'

The phone rang again.

'Sorry, I'd better take this,' Cathy said. 'It's my husband again. Hello? You can't manage to use the rolling pin?'

Mrs Oatcake flicked her eyes heavenwards and smirked.

'So you've squidged it into the dish with your fingers and you want to know if I think that'll work?'

Mrs Oatcake shook her head.

'It might.' Cathy shrugged. 'Yes, I think you're correct, it might spread out a bit during the cooking process.

'Yes, your tutor was right when she told you cooking is a mysterious process.'

'Chemistry with a dash of magic,' Mrs Oatcake added helpfully.

'Indeed, did you hear that, Pete? Mrs Oatcake says cooking is chemistry with a dash of — ah, you heard.

'And, yes, it's also true some things don't look too good until they're cooked but you can be pleasantly surprised once they come out of the oven.

'Like scones, exactly.

'Bye, Pete. Many apologies, Mrs Oat-cake. Do go on. You were telling me which authors you admire?'

★ ★ ★

As Cathy left Mrs Oatcake's house, on her way to tackle the church flowers, she rang Pete to check on the progress of the quiche.

'You had to start again? Why?'

'I hadn't quite finished making the filling. You remember when you saw the eggs on the side, still in their shells?

'I wasn't sure what to do with them or how many to use. I noticed the pot of cream on the counter, too. I'd forgotten to add some.

'At least, I think I'd forgotten — to be honest, I wasn't sure. And I didn't know if I should add some seasoning.'

'But I still don't understand why you had to start again. Why couldn't you look at the recipe? Wait a minute, please, Pete, would you? I'm getting on the bus.

'OK. Sitting down now. Fire away.'

'The recipe was inside the dish, printed on the china, and I'd covered it with pastry.

'I tried to peel the pastry sheet back, but because it wasn't a sheet, more of a cobbled-together lumpy mess, once I had the stuff in my hands it sort of slipped through my fingers and fell on the floor.

'Our tutor told us not to use ingredients that had been on the floor.'

Cathy decided not to mention that earlier, when they'd been in the kitchen together at home, she'd noticed Pete pick up a piece of bacon he'd dropped on the floor and add it to the filling.

It wouldn't be helpful, she felt, under the circumstances.

'Poor you,' she said instead. 'But what a great idea, to start again but to photograph the recipe inside the dish on your phone before you lined it with fresh pastry.

'Hang on, I've got to get off at this stop. What did you just say?'

'I couldn't read the recipe on my

phone because it was too small. I should have worn my reading glasses. And when I tried to enlarge it, I deleted it.'

'If I were you,' Cathy said, in the kindly, patient tone she'd previously reserved for talking to five-year-olds in the classroom, 'I'd look up another recipe, on the internet. See if you can find one using roughly the same ingredients.'

'Thanks. I was sure you'd know what to do.'

Pete rang off and Cathy hurried into the church to begin sorting and snipping, helping to create lovely floral displays to gladden the hearts of the congregation.

Cathy was halfway through her pampering session in Jane Hair, with the junior raking conditioner through Cathy's thick locks with her red talons in an attempt to give her a relaxing scalp massage, when she realised Pete must have been successful in his cooking.

There had been no more desperate phone calls — surely a good sign?

★ ★ ★

Cathy felt all was well with the world as she left the salon, her lustrous curls bouncing around her shoulders.

Mrs Oatcake seemed to have enjoyed her visit, the flower arranging at the church had gone smoothly, Pete would have the meal ready by the time she got home and she felt like a million dollars with her new hair-do.

She didn't have to wait long for the bus and was home within minutes.

'Hello!' she called. 'I'm back . . . eek! What's that smell?'

Cathy flew straight to the kitchen and flung open the window to let the stench of charcoal escape.

'What's been going on? Argh! I've stepped in something sticky on the floor. What is it?'

'Pastry. My first attempt. I tried to clear it up but I might have missed a bit.'

Pete pointed to a tea towel lying on the side, encrusted with grey dry lumps.

'And what's the burning smell?'

'The second attempt.'

'Oh, Pete! What happened?'

'I forgot to set the timer. You know the book I've been wanting to finish for ages? The one about Egypt?

'I thought I'd read a bit of it while the quiche was cooking, but no sooner was I visiting the pyramids of Giza, dreaming of the days of the great Pharaohs, than I fell fast asleep on the sofa.

'The smoke alarm woke me in the end. As I say, I should have set the timer. I know that now.'

'Never mind. Accidents happen.'

Cathy tried hard not to giggle as Pete walked across the floor and retrieved a crisp, black object from the bin, about the size of a thick dinner plate.

'Here's the quiche,' he said solemnly. 'It's burnt.'

'No kidding!' Cathy laughed. 'Sorry, Pete, but you have to see the funny side!'

Pete's face creased into a smile as he lobbed the ruined quiche back into the swing-top bin.

'So, do you fancy going out for supper?'

Travel Companions

'Are you sure you didn't make a mistake, Allegra? About the engagement ring?' Holly held on firmly to the car handle as the taxi swung round a corner at speed.

'No. Vanessa was wearing Zack's grandmother's ring. I should be able to recognise it, if anyone can.'

Allegra slumped in her seat. The tour had been a triumph and now they were on their way to the airport to fly back to England.

Maestro Rostopovsky had attended all three concerts the orchestra and choir had performed, but in the audience.

The medics had thought it best for him not to over-exert himself. He'd been working too hard, on one tour after another, conducting and rehearsing all over the globe. He was now off on a luxury cruise and a well-deserved break.

After stepping into the breach so ably, Zack's reputation as a conductor was even better than before. He'd been in the press, praised to the skies.

'You'd think Zack would be getting quite big-headed with all these fantastic reviews,' Holly said, scanning the newspaper, 'except it's not his style.'

'No,' Allegra agreed. 'I could say a lot of things about Zack, but I would never accuse him of being boastful or showing off.'

'Sorry. I didn't mean to mention him.'

'Unavoidable in this case,' Allegra replied. 'He's been amazing, with the orchestra. But it changes nothing between us. He's still engaged to Vanessa.'

'Do you mind about her? I mean, you never said why you broke off your engagement, even to me, your best friend.'

Allegra looked away.

'He started looking for someone — oh, I shouldn't say because he asked me not to. But heaven knows, after all this time, I can't see what harm it could do.'

'No,' Holly warned, 'don't break a confidence. Whatever it was, do you think you made the right decision?'

'I thought so at the time,' Allegra said,

'because he wasn't ready to commit. There was too much else from his past he needed to sort out.

'But now,' she continued, so softly that Holly had to strain to catch her words, 'I suspect if I'd acted in a more mature way, maybe I could have helped him. I shouldn't have left him to deal with it on his own.'

'Here we are, ladies,' the taxi driver interrupted. '*Aeropuerto*! Now you fly back to England and your beloved rain.'

Holly laughed as she paid the driver.

'We don't love the rain, we get used to it! Thank you, yes, you, too, and good-bye.'

'We need to run,' Allegra said. 'We'll be late — come on, Holly!'

'There's plenty of time.'

'No, we need to get going!' Allegra urged, rushing forward, with the wheels of her case spinning madly as she ran into the terminal.

She had just seen Zack jumping out of a nearby taxi.

'Coming!' Holly panted as she raced after her friend. 'Though I don't know what the fuss is.'

She caught up with Allegra at the check-in desk.

'You don't need to be frightened of Zack. You've been with him all week.'

'That was mostly in a crowd,' Allegra qualified.

She wasn't ready to have any sort of personal conversation with Zack. Besides, the airport was reminding her of Zack's new fiancée, Vanessa.

The ruby ring had looked gorgeous on her finger. Her hands were shapely and elegant, with beautifully manicured, very long, nails.

Hang on! She couldn't be a musician, could she, with extravagant nails? Zack always said he loved Allegra even more because of their shared passion for music. She was sure he would only be interested in a musician. He could have changed, of course.

Or perhaps Vanessa was a singer. Singers often had lovely long nails, not needing their fingers to fly nimbly over an instrument.

But Zack often used to make jokes about singers, Allegra reminded herself, recalling his favourite.

'How do you know when a soprano is at your door? She can't find the key and doesn't know when to come in.'

Allegra felt a giggle bubble up, a giggle she hastily subdued as she realised Zack was right behind them in the queue.

'Flying back to England?' Holly asked.

'Yes,' Zack replied.

His voice, his beautiful, silky, deep, gravelly voice. Allegra breathed slowly then forced herself to turn round and greet him.

'Hi!'

His eyes. Meltingly attractive, chocolate brown with a tinge of dark green.

'Did you pack this bag yourself?' the check-in assistant asked Allegra. 'Any knives? Sharp objects?'

Only Cupid's arrow piercing her heart again. That must count as a sharp object, surely?

Of all the coincidences, Zack happened to have been allocated the seat on the plane next to Allegra. He had the window seat, with Allegra in the middle and Holly on the aisle.

Allegra thought about trying to manoeuvre Holly to sit in the middle, but instead decided to embrace her fate.

'Enjoy the concerts?' Zack asked.

'Yes.'

'Where are you working next?'

'London.'

'How have you been?'

'Look, we're taking off! I love this bit.' Allegra stared across Zack and saw the yellow and brown ground disappearing.

'We'll have to get used to an English autumn again,' Holly said. 'Rain, as the taxi driver kindly reminded us.'

There followed a polite conversation between the three of them about the weather, before Holly started flicking through a magazine and Allegra pulled out her Kindle.

'You haven't turned the page,' Zack said to Allegra after a while. 'How do you turn the page on a Kindle, anyway?'

Allegra showed him the button on the side, wondering why he'd been watching her.

'Maybe it was a very interesting page and I was reading it several times over,' she suggested.

'Unlikely, but possible.' Zack smiled. 'Tell me, though, how have you been? How's work, and how are your parents?'

'All fine, thank you. I know how your work's been going because I've read about you in the papers. You're quite famous now! I'm so pleased for you.'

Zack looked down at his hands.

'Thank you.'

Allegra decided to be bold. Where was the harm? It wasn't as if he could run away.

'I'm pleased to see your personal life's good, too.'

'My what?'

'Vanessa. Your fiancée?'

Zack laughed, throwing his head back hard against the seat. This caused the lady directly behind him to admonish him.

71

'Steady, that's my coffee you're spill-ing!'

That made him laugh even more. Finally, he wiped the tears from his eyes with a handkerchief embroidered with crotchets and quavers, at the sight of which Allegra gave a sudden gasp of recognition.

'Allegra, I'm not engaged to Vanessa, nor anyone else. What gave you that idea?'

'The ring. Your grandmother's ring.'

'Ah.' Zack inspected his nails. 'You noticed that. After you — we, I mean . . .'

'After I threw the ring back at you and broke our engagement,' Allegra supplied.

After I made the most stupid idiotic mistake of my life, one I'll regret until my dying day.

'Yes. Our broken engagement.' Zack looked out of the window.

'Why was she wearing it, then?' Allegra demanded.

'My grandmother gave me the ring, as her elder grandson, to give to my intended wife. But after we split up, I didn't want to have the ring any more.

'I couldn't imagine giving it to anyone else, not after you. So I talked to my grandmother and she thought it would be best to give it to Joe.'

'Your brother? So Vanessa must be . . .'

'Engaged to my brother, Joe, correct. They're planning a spring wedding.

'We were on our way to join Joe in Switzerland for a few days' holiday when you saw us. Not a complete holiday for me; you know what I'm like. I took some music with me, hoping to get time to study a new piece I'm conducting soon.'

Zack hadn't changed, Allegra thought. He was never without his precious music case, bulging with masterpieces.

'Joe had gone out ahead of Vanessa and me,' Zack continued, 'because of some business he had there. When you saw me with Vanessa, we were travelling out to join him at a lodge in the mountains.

'The three of us intended to spend a few days hiking.'

'But you called her 'honey'.'

Allegra still couldn't quite accept Zack's version of events — it was so very different from the painful narrative she'd spun in her mind, torturing herself with jealous thoughts.

And would the glamorous creature she'd seen with Zack be tempted to go hiking?

'Honey? What? Oh, yes, I believe I did.'

Zack started laughing again.

'Vanessa's an actress and singer and has recently been in a Broadway show — in which she played the part of a young woman called Honey.

'Joe and her friends keep calling her Honey and it's become a bit of a joke. No doubt we'll be calling her Christine soon because she's . . .'

' . . .going to be in 'Phantom Of The Opera'?' Relief flooded through Allegra.

She squeezed her coffee cup so hard the brittle plastic crackled and split in her grasp.

'You always did have strong hands,' Zack remarked. 'Lucky you'd finished your coffee!'

Vanessa wasn't engaged to Zack — he was still single! She wasn't even his girlfriend, but was going to be his sister-in-law.

'I'm going to the ladies,' Holly interrupted as she undid her seatbelt.

'I'll come with you!' Allegra said.

As the two friends queued in the narrow aisle, Allegra grabbed Holly's arm.

'He's still got the handkerchief — the one with crotchets and quavers!'

'The one you embroidered for him?'

'Yes!' Allegra's face split into a broad grin.

'I couldn't help overhearing,' Holly said. 'So he's not engaged. Welcome news?'

'Absolutely!'

'Absolutely what?' a rich bass voice boomed behind Allegra.

'Boris!' she said with a start. 'You gave me a fright, creeping up on me! I didn't even know you were on the flight.'

'Yet here I am.'

Leaning forward, he gave Allegra a

75

massive hug.

'Sorry, I'm too broad to reach over to you, Holly,' he apologised. 'They couldn't make these aisles narrower if they tried.'

'I'll forgive you this time, Boris,' Holly promised.

Boris pursed his lips and blew Holly a gentle kiss.

'Lovely to see you two ladies. I say, I don't suppose either of you are free next Wednesday, are you?

'I've got spare tickets for Covent Garden looking for a good home, and I'd be honoured if you could both join me.'

'Sounds fun,' Holly enthused. 'Here, give me your number and we can get in touch.'

'Yes, lovely.' Allegra nodded.

'Super! Can't wait,' Boris said.

Allegra remembered when she'd been to see 'Carmen' with Zack — he adored Covent Garden and one of his greatest ambitions was to conduct an opera there.

She looked down the aisle towards their seats. Zack was standing up, staring at her.

Was it her imagination, or was he glowering?

Oh, no — perhaps he'd seen Boris's rather over-enthusiastic embrace, then put two and two together and made five?

Just as she'd thought they were getting on so well together . . .

Sunday Lunch

'Did you put any water with those vegetables,' Cathy asked, 'before you put the
saucepan on a high heat?'

'Of course,' Pete answered. 'I'm
insulted that you think I didn't!

'I only put a tiny bit, mind you, because
my tutor said it's much better to gently
steam the veg. It keeps the vitamins and
nutrients intact.'

Cathy's eyebrows shot up.

'What?' Pete asked. 'Why are you
checking up on me?'

Cathy nodded at the saucepan which
was almost jumping off the hob, it was
so hot.

There was a hissing noise and steam
was whooshing out, lifting the lid as it
escaped.

'Maybe a bit more water?'

Pete rushed the pan to the sink and
gave it a blast of water from the tap.
Pieces of singed broccoli and shredded,
pale yellow carrot bobbed miserably to

the surface.

'The water pressure's high today,' Pete remarked. 'I meant to put a tiny dribble of water in, but . . .'

'Never mind,' Cathy said. 'But you have put the veg on very early.'

She looked at Pete's expression.

'In my humble opinion.'

'No, you're right,' Pete said. 'My cookery teacher said it's best to wait until your guests arrive before starting.

'She told us a few jokes about how people used to put the Christmas veg on to cook in November! Shame I didn't remember before I lit the gas.'

'Nothing to worry about,' Cathy said, 'We've got time to cook some more. There's plenty left — bottom of the fridge in the cooler drawer.'

Pete grabbed a tea towel and twisted it as if trying to strangle a thought.

He might be mulling over the quiche episode, Cathy thought.

At length he sighed.

'I'm beginning to think cooking's not my thing.'

Cathy tried desperately to think of something encouraging to say.

'Have you thought of joining a book group?' she suggested eventually.

It sounded pretty lame, even to her ears.

Pete gave a lop-sided grin.

'I prefer reading to cooking, for sure, but I was wanting to do something in a group, not indulge in a solitary occupation like reading.

'I couldn't do that all the time — it would drive me nuts! That's why I miss teaching — I long for the fun of the classroom, the kids, the banter.

'Hearing them screaming for joy at break time and seeing their faces glowing with pleasure when you explain something to them and they suddenly get it.'

'You don't miss the marking, the record keeping, the endless meetings and so on, do you?' Cathy asked gently.

'I do not!' Pete shuddered. 'It was a huge responsibility, being Head of English at Byron High School. No way would I want to go back to that.

'Thanks for reminding me why I left! Maybe cooking's not so bad. At least it's better than golf.'

Cathy's shoulders lowered a notch. She knew Pete was finding retirement challenging, but was relieved he had no plans to go back to teaching.

He had found the last few years of his career stressful and she had no desire to see him that unhappy and tired again. Going back to teaching wouldn't be the right thing at all — for him.

Pete grinned.

'Want to help me peel more carrots?'

★ ★ ★

Their first guest arrived soon afterwards. It was Allegra, back from her trip to Barcelona and longing to see her parents.

She had time for a flying visit, arriving for Sunday lunch and leaving on Monday to the London flat she shared with Holly.

'Good drive down, darling?' Cathy

asked as she folded Allegra in her warm embrace.

Privately, she thought her thinner than ever and didn't like the way she looked so drawn. What had been going on?

Cathy hoped Zack hadn't been upsetting her again.

'All fine, Mum. Hi, Dad, great to see you. Something smells delicious. Roast lamb!

'Is that your doing, Dad? I've been hearing all about your new course from Mum. You'll be setting up a restaurant chain soon!'

'Ah,' Pete said, 'your mother's been helping me. I'll tell you the story of the vegetables later.

'Let's go and sit down, while we wait for our other guest.'

'I hope you don't mind, dear,' Cathy said, 'but I asked Maeve to join us.'

'Why would I mind? I always enjoy seeing her, though sometimes I feel I'm back at school! I still think of her as Mrs Turnbull, not Maeve.'

Cathy and Maeve had taught at the

same school, which was how the two had met and become firm friends, and the friendship had continued even when Maeve had been appointed headmistress.

Cathy often thought Maeve was like an unofficial godmother to Allegra. With no children of her own, she had taken a very strong interest in Allegra's welfare.

★ ★ ★

Half an hour later Pete, Cathy, Allegra and Maeve were eating a delicious roast dinner.

'Mum!' Allegra sighed with pleasure. 'This is perfect! But I'm not sure I'll have room for pudding.'

'Superb,' Maeve commented, 'as always! How do you get the roast potatoes so fluffy?'

'Pete advised me on those,' Cathy replied. 'A top tip from his cookery lesson.'

'Ah, yes,' Maeve said. 'I've yet to hear all the details about this course.'

Pudding was a massive apple crumble, served with whipped cream.

'Or you can have yoghurt,' Cathy said. 'Maeve?'

Maeve shrieked with laughter.

'Are you suggesting yoghurt because it's low calorie?' she said. 'It's a bit late, after everything else I've scoffed today!

'No, Allegra, of course I'm not offended by what your mother said. I think it's hilarious!'

Cathy looked at Maeve and felt a rush of affection for her friend. Maeve could be tactless but she never took offence.

'Cream,' Maeve said, 'Definitely cream! And you, Allegra, must have cream, lashings of it.

'Come on, now, you're looking a bit peaky — get some meat on your bones, girl!'

Maeve reached across the table and spooned a generous helping of cream on to Allegra's apple pie.

'Mrs Turnbull!' Allegra protested. 'I mean, Maeve! No! I haven't got room.'

'Now you can tell me all about your

trip to Barcelona,' Maeve said, leaning forward eagerly. 'Spill the beans! What was it like meeting Zack after all this time?'

'Mum!' Allegra said. 'I can't believe you've been talking . . .'

'She hasn't, my dear,' Maeve said. 'I follow the news, don't I? It was in the paper, how Zack saved the show by stepping in at the last minute.

'Quite a career opportunity!'

'I don't think he saw it as a career opportunity,' Allegra said. 'More a way he could help out.'

'Nonsense,' Maeve retorted. 'Of course he had an eye on the main chance — he'd be a fool not to.

'And who's this Boris person the news referred to? Boris the bass?'

'He's the singer who took over,' Allegra explained. 'He's very charming. Larger than life personality and amazingly kind.

'He has a fabulous voice and he's not bad at conducting, either.'

'He loaned Allegra his violin,' Cathy added, anxious to steer the conversation away from Zack. 'Remember I mentioned it had been stolen?'

'No result yet from the police,' Pete added.

'Shocking! They can't be as efficient as our police here,' Maeve said. 'When my purse was stolen last year, taken from my bag by some sort of low life and in broad daylight, too, it was found in the road and handed in by a good Samaritan.'

'Yes, with all your cards and money still inside,' Pete said. 'I wondered at the time if perhaps you'd merely dropped your purse.'

Maeve raised her hands up.

'I'd never be so careless,' she said. 'It was stolen — beyond dispute!'

Cathy smothered a smile. Maeve was completely impossible at times, but she was a dear friend.

She had been a listening ear for Cathy when Allegra had broken up with Zack in what had seemed to Cathy and Pete such an unexpected way.

They had been looking forward to

welcoming Zack into their family and had found the break-up both shocking and incomprehensible in equal measure.

No point in raking up the past, though, was there?

What was done was done, and hopefully it wouldn't be too long before Allegra found someone else, someone she could care for as deeply.

'This Boris,' Maeve said to Allegra, 'tell me more about him.'

'I'm seeing him next week, actually,' Allegra replied. 'He's taking Holly and me to the opera at Covent Garden on Wednesday.

'He has a friend in the chorus there, a tenor, and he managed to get three tickets for the first night of 'The Barber Of Seville'.'

'Super!' Cathy said.

'I can see you winking at Mum, Maeve!' Allegra said. 'Boris and I are friends, nothing more, although I wouldn't be surprised if Boris wasn't a bit keen on Holly, truth be told.'

The corners of Mauve's mouth turned

down a little as she digested this, but she soon recovered.

'What about his friend, the tenor?' she demanded.

Dear Maeve, Cathy thought. She simply never gave up!

She felt the same — of course she'd like to see Allegra settled. But interfering wasn't the way.

Cathy might have to have a word with Maeve next time they were alone. They were due to have one of their special days out in London next Tuesday — that might be a good occasion to have a heart to heart with her.

Every so often, Cathy and Maeve caught an early train from Bath up to Paddington and spent the day together looking at art galleries and hitting the shops, sometimes managing to catch a matinée at a West End theatre.

It was a very welcome break for Cathy from her usual round of duties and she was thoroughly looking forward to it.

'Coffee?' Pete suggested. 'Something I am good at preparing. No, you ladies sit still while I clear the table.

'I'll load up the dishwasher and bring your coffee through. Relax!'

'You've got a good one there,' Maeve said as soon as Pete had left the room.

'That's not what you said last week,' Cathy argued, 'when you told me to tackle him about the mysterious text.'

'What's this?' Allegra asked.

'Nothing at all,' Maeve said. 'I made a silly snap judgement and your mother, quite rightly, told me that what I was suspecting was laughable.

'But she was worried in a different way because, as you know, your father . . . Oh, me and my big mouth, I always make things worse!'

Cathy explained to Allegra about the text from the lady at the library in charge of adult education.

Then the women reminisced about Pete's retirement phases and before long the three of them were giggling at the absurdity of it all.

Pete staggered in with a tray of coffee and joined in the merriment by recounting the tale of his cooking disasters.

'The quiche wasn't even recognisable,' he said. 'It was a solid black disc, like a Frisbee. As for the veg this morning, words fail me!'

'Enough, Pete!' Maeve begged. 'I can't stop giggling; it's so funny.'

'It's going to be almost impossible to clean the saucepan,' Pete said. 'I've left it to soak, but I don't hold out much hope.'

'I think I can hear the house phone. Don't worry, I'll get it; stay there, Pete, and enjoy your coffee.' Cathy rushed out to the hall.

'It's for you, Allegra,' she said a minute later, popping her head back round the door. 'A call from London.'

Cathy closed the door of the dining-room as Allegra took her call in the hall.

'Is it Boris?' Maeve asked.

'No,' Cathy said.

'Shame. He could have been ringing to ask Allegra out to dinner with Holly and his tenor friend.'

'Don't get carried away, Maeve,' Pete

said, smiling. 'Who is it, love? You've gone rather quiet.'

'It's Zack,' Cathy said. 'He said he wanted to talk to Allegra about something important.'

Maeve twisted her napkin in her fingers and Pete looked down at the tablecloth.

As the room fell silent, they could hear Allegra's soft tones even through the closed door.

'Yes, all right, Zack. Tomorrow it is. Six o'clock. Thank you.'

The Music Lesson

Allegra was aiming to reach her flat in Croydon around two p.m. on Monday. She'd had a late leisurely breakfast with her parents, then had set off with many promises to keep in touch.

She suspected they'd heard her on the phone to Zack yesterday. They'd been walking on eggshells this morning, unable to ask her about the call.

Allegra swerved to avoid a rabbit bouncing along, oblivious to danger. She fiddled with radio controls until she found something worth listening to. Ah, Bach!

As she drove past Stonehenge Allegra's heart beat faster. She'd visited the site with Zack. It was a memorable day, full of love and hope, of plans for the future.

Allegra shivered as she recollected Zack holding her hand, marvelling at the huge ancient stones full of history and secrets.

Once, she'd stumbled and he'd caught

her before she fell, enfolding her in his arms.

She swerved again, this time not because of a rabbit, and decided to pull into the next lay-by. Car safely parked, the tears began to flow and once started, she couldn't seem to stop.

'I still love him!' Allegra whispered, sobbing. 'I don't think I can face seeing him this evening without telling him how I feel, but it would be all wrong.'

After a while she blew her nose and checked her face in the mirror. Her car rocked slightly as the traffic whooshed past and she realised she felt able to continue on her journey.

'Mirror, signal, manoeuvre,' she chanted as she pulled back on to the road. 'Full speed ahead! If I don't get a move on, my violin pupil will be at the flat for their lesson before I am!'

In addition to her freelance orchestral commitments, Allegra had eight violin pupils. They had to be flexible to fit in around her schedule, which was never the same from week to week.

She particularly enjoyed working with youngsters, passing on what she knew and sharing her passion for music.

Allegra was prone to saying she learned far more from her pupils than they ever learned from her. When she had said that to one of her pupils, the ten-year-old had given a cheeky smile.

'Why does my mum pay you, then? Shouldn't you pay me?'

Allegra had laughed, taking the remark in the spirit it was given.

When Allegra finally reached London she had to drive round for a good 10 minutes looking for a space to park before she could make her way upstairs to the top-floor flat of Elgin Court.

There was a note on the kitchen table from Holly.

Out at a recording session at Abbey Road Studios — see you later!

Allegra gave the sitting-room a quick once-over, hiding various clothes waiting to be ironed and tidying the enormous pile of books and magazines.

She took Boris's violin out and tuned

it ready for the lesson.

As the doorbell went, she spotted a couple of abandoned coffee cups and plates and hastily popped them into the tiny kitchen adjacent to the main room.

Within minutes of her arrival Allegra's pupil, Cassie, was cheerfully playing 'How Much Is That Doggy In The Window?' while Cassie's mother listened proudly from the sofa.

'You're really coming on!' Allegra enthused. 'You're much more in tune than when you played last week. Well done!

'Remember to hold the bow more like this.' She demonstrated. 'More gracefully, not like a spear or a stick.'

'But it is a stick,' Cassie said, her eyebrows knitting together.

'It is, you're quite right,' Allegra said, 'but the sound will be even sweeter if you try it this way . . . and this.'

'It definitely sounds better,' Cassie's mum said. 'Mind if I take a picture of your hand, Allegra? I'd like to help Cassie get the proper position at home.'

'I was about to make the same suggestion,' Allegra replied.

'What's that?' Cassie asked, pointing.

'Something very sweet!' Allegra pulled a tiny teddy bear on a loop of ribbon out from Boris's violin case.

'Why is it in your case?'

'I've borrowed this violin — it belongs to a friend of mine.'

One with a soft centre, Allegra thought.

'My violin was taken — stolen — in Spain.'

'I'm sorry to hear that,' Cassie's mum said.

'But why does he keep a teddy in his case? Your friend?' Cassie persisted.

'I don't know,' Allegra said. 'Maybe he's a very sweet man who still loves teddies.'

Cassie looked satisfied with the answer, much to Allegra's relief.

There was a limit to the number of 'why' questions she felt up to answering each lesson.

'I'll mention your violin to my husband,' Cassie's mum said. 'He's in the police so he might be able to help.'

'Thank you,' Allegra said. 'The police in Spain don't seem to have had much luck yet. I'd be interested to know if your husband thinks we should be doing anything else.'

'You should hire a private detective!' Cassie suggested, excited.

Allegra smiled.

'I've shared pictures and a description of the instrument as extensively as I can, but beyond that I'm not sure what I can realistically do.'

'Leave it with me. I'll see what my other half says and I'll text you. OK?'

★ ★ ★

Once Cassie and her mother had left, Allegra felt yet another pang at the loss of her treasured violin.

Boris had recommended a description and pictures of the violin and bow should be circulated, as an instrument reported as stolen would be more difficult to sell on.

Everyone in the orchestra and choir had helped with this, using social media to contact musicians throughout the world.

The story had also appeared in the local press in Spain, with a picture of Allegra in full concert dress holding her violin, taken in happier times.

There was nothing more she could do at the moment.

Realising she didn't have long before she needed to leave for her appointment with Zack, she ran into her bedroom and started rifling through her clothes. Very soon the floor was littered with discarded garments.

She scolded herself—it was ridiculous to worry about how she might appear to Zack. As if he would be interested!

Rationalising this did not stop the panic threatening to engulf her.

They had arranged to meet because he'd suggested it was time they got together as friends, and she'd agreed on the phone that it would be a good thing to be friends.

But her whole body was screaming out that friendship wasn't what she had in mind. She wanted more.

She wanted her Zack, her true love, back where he belonged, at the centre of her life.

Just Friends

In the pizzeria Allegra sat waiting for Zack, fiddling with her necklace. She wore a dress he'd often admired. It was a greenish-blue colour, loosely fitted and flowing.

She saw him the moment he appeared at the doorway, the light reflecting on his shiny dark curls.

'Sorry!' he said. 'The rehearsal ran late, followed by trouble with the bus. Have you ordered?'

'I didn't know what you wanted,' Allegra pointed out.

'Same as I always used to have.' Zack grinned. 'Thick crust, four seasons with extra cheese.'

Allegra smiled.

'I thought you might have refined your taste since we last ate here.'

'No chance!'

Zack looked across the table, eyes twinkling.

'It's good to see you. I've often hoped

we could meet like this, as friends. There's no reason why not, is there?'

'Yes, because I'm in love with you and can't settle for mere friendship!' Allegra wanted to scream at him.

She was saved from potential embarrassment by the arrival of the waiter.

★ ★ ★

'So, how did it go?' Holly asked later.

'We had a lovely meal,' Allegra said, 'but he wasn't the same. Correction, we weren't the same.

'He was polite and attentive, very charming, with lots of amusing stories and gossip about the music business, but I felt I hardly knew him any more.'

'It's been a long time,' Holly said. 'He must have had a reason to want to meet up with you again. Did he want to talk about what had happened between you?'

'Yes, he brought it up straight away, almost as if it was a task he had to get over.'

Allegra stirred her cocoa and put her

legs up on the sofa. She and Holly were both in their dressing-gowns, relaxing in the sitting-room with their bedtime drinks.

'He was very matter of fact about it. He said that break-ups happen, it was common, and he understood my reasons for wanting to end our engagement.

'He said he knew we weren't suited because of what happened when we split, but he'd always be fond of me and I'd have a special place in his heart, as a friend.'

'Not special enough to get re-engaged?'

Allegra bit her lip.

'It didn't seem to have crossed his mind to rekindle our romance. This was more about closing the door on the chapter.

'I felt I was a loose end that had to be adjusted, or removed, before he could carry on with his life.

'It was almost as if someone had told him he needed to meet up with me again, to make sure there were no hard feelings.'

'Don't look at me.' Holly shrugged. 'I would never try to interfere. I know from experience how it can backfire.'

She took a sip of her drink.

'I know you can't tell me why you broke up with him and, as I've said before, I would never expect you to break his confidence, but it is hard to understand why you broke up, not knowing the facts.'

Allegra thought back to the moment she'd thrown the engagement ring at Zack, the culmination of a lot of emotion and drama.

'To make a long story short, he had told me something about his past,' Allegra said. 'I didn't think it should have been a secret, and I told him so.

'He was becoming obsessed with it; it was eating away at him. He said he couldn't marry me until he'd found the answer.

'It made me very concerned that he thought we shouldn't get married until he'd sorted this out. I wanted to help him, to advise and support him, but he wouldn't hear of it. He said it was his situation, his problem; nothing to do with me.

'All of a sudden I realised we were too young to commit to each other. It was all too rushed, and so I behaved in the most childish and hurtful way, by rejecting him. What I wouldn't give to go back in time!'

Holly sighed.

'It doesn't mean you can't fix things now,' she offered.

'We're not the same people and what we had is well and truly over, at least as far as he's concerned,' Allegra said. 'I saw his face when we said goodbye outside the restaurant. It had relief written all over it.

'There wasn't even a hug, let alone a peck on the cheek. He had come with a mission, to smooth over any possible unpleasantness between us. I was a mistake from his past he came to visit, to check on, and now he's happy.'

'You could have got this completely wrong,' Holly said. 'You do know that? It wouldn't be the first time you've misread a situation where Zack's concerned.'

'You mean at Gatwick, when I thought he was engaged to Vanessa? That was a different situation,' Allegra declared.

'Nevertheless, consider the possibility you've misread the situation again,' Holly argued. 'When Zack asked you to meet for a meal, he might not have been trying to close a door, but attempting to make a fresh start.

'Did you ask him about this mystery?'

'Yes,' Allegra said. 'He said he'd made progress, but the way he said it made me feel it wasn't anything to do with me and he didn't want to share details.

'I felt as excluded as I'd done all those years ago, when we were engaged. Zack always was a very private person.'

'It almost sounds as if he were checking up on you out of concern, to see if you were all right.'

'I think he was. And I let him think I was fine,' Allegra said sadly. 'If he knew . . .'

'Maybe you should have been more open with him. Told him how you felt,'

Holly suggested.

'I didn't want to make it all about me. He obviously still has a lot to sort out, and why should I want to burden him with feelings he doesn't want to hear about?'

'It's late,' Holly said as she tidied away their cups. 'Things will seem better in the morning. I'm back in the recording studio tomorrow. What have you got on?'

'Nothing until the afternoon, thank goodness,' Allegra said as she yawned. 'A rehearsal, and concert in the evening.'

'I've heard from Boris, confirming our tickets for Wednesday.' Holly smiled.

'He's so kind,' Allegra said as she switched off lights in the sitting-room, 'and he seems pretty keen on you.'

'I think you'll find it's you he's keen on.'

Allegra gaped. She was sure Holly and Boris were made for each other.

'I mean it!' Holly said. 'You can't see it because of your feelings for Zack. Remember how helpful Boris was in Spain, when your violin was stolen?

'And lending you his violin — above and beyond the call of duty, surely?'

'He's just a lovely guy. I'm sure he would have done the same for anyone. It's good to know I've got friends like you, Holly, and Boris, looking out for me.

'It helps with my feelings for Zack. I'll soon be able to put all this behind me.'

Despite saying this, Allegra knew her feelings for Zack showed no signs of abating.

In fact, having seen him so many times in the last week, her feelings were growing ever more intense, if such a thing were possible.

As she lay in her bed that night, her mind went back to the day of their engagement.

It had been a perfect summer's day — they'd been out for a picnic in the local park, eating hard-boiled eggs and sandwiches, with a flask of tea, fragrant strawberries and fresh apricots.

They'd sprawled under a willow tree, relaxed and happy in each other's company, no need for words, contented and floating in happiness.

'Will you marry me?' they'd both said together, then pulled towards each other, kissing and laughing, deciding how to tell everyone, and planning for the future.

That had been the turning point, Allegra thought. Things had started to go wrong on the day they'd became engaged.

Zack seemed to become troubled, weighed down by something. He kept talking about what they would do when they were married; about where they were to live, children, jobs and so on.

Allegra, meanwhile, was content to enjoy being engaged and didn't want to make lots of important decisions now. She thought they could face things together, if and when circumstances changed.

She saw it was important to Zack to have firm plans and tried to understand and accommodate his more controlling approach to life, but she found it hard.

She confided in her mother, but Cathy said everyone was different and that marriage meant give and take — it would all work out.

One day Allegra tried to explain to Zack that she was confident things would work out naturally — they didn't need to make plans about family and so on.

Zack shouted and said it wasn't enough, you had to plan, otherwise terrible situations happened. You only had to look at what had happened to him.

Once he started talking, Allegra thought he would never stop. He poured out his story to her, all his worries, his fears.

How important it was to him to have things be different when he had a family, to make sure everything was OK.

Zack had been adopted as a baby. His mother had been a young, unmarried nurse who had trusted a man who didn't prove himself worthy. She'd been abandoned and felt the best option for her unborn child was to put it up for adoption.

'Zack, I didn't even know you'd been adopted,' Allegra said. 'Why did you wait until now to tell me this?'

Zack's face was a picture of misery and Allegra put her arms round him in a trice.

'Thank you for telling me,' she whispered. 'It must have been a hard secret to keep.'

Zack said he'd had the happiest of childhoods with his adopted parents. To their great joy, after thinking they couldn't have children and adopting Zack they'd managed to produce his brother Joe just one year after Zack's arrival.

The two boys grew up as close as brothers can be, sharing everything except looks. Zack was tall and dark, whereas Joe was shorter, with blond hair and blue eyes.

If anyone noticed how different the two brothers were, they didn't comment on it.

The family chose not to talk about the adoption outside their family circle, as if Zack and Joe were natural brothers, which was exactly how they felt. They thought it was for the best.

When Zack fell in love with Allegra he had begun, almost for the first time, to contemplate his own beginnings.

'I keep thinking about my natural mother,' he told her. 'I want to know where she is, find out if she wants to see me, if she ever regretted giving me away.'

★ ★ ★

Allegra sat up in bed, realising she wasn't going to be able to get to sleep with these memories swirling round and round.

She got up and padded to the kitchen to make some tea. Waiting for the kettle to boil, she relived the next stage of the story — when she and Zack had split up.

'I wasn't understanding enough,' she whispered. 'I could have been mature about it all, but instead, I was thinking about myself.

'I wanted him to come to terms with his adoption instantly, so we could get married and have our happy-ever-after.

111

I didn't give poor Zack the support he deserved.'

She remembered the day she'd gone round to see Zack, having decided he needed a few home truths instead of wallowing in self-pity.

He'd been given to a lovely family — what was his problem?

Allegra groaned as she recollected how thoughtless and selfish she'd been, showing such a complete lack of understanding.

The day before, Allegra had been at her parents' house in Bath and Maeve had dropped by, as she often did.

Allegra found herself telling Maeve all about Zack acting oddly, without telling her why. He'd asked her not to share the news, even with her family, about him being adopted.

This was just one more reason she felt he was being unreasonable, because it was so difficult not to tell anyone at all!

Maeve gave Allegra some of her usual advice, coloured by her somewhat jaundiced view of the male of the species, and as she confronted Zack Allegra found Maeve's words in her mouth.

'You need to sort out your priorities, Zack!' she yelled.

She took her engagement ring off and waved it under Zack's nose.

'Maybe we shouldn't get married!'

As she fled, Allegra remembered, too late, how desperately proud Zack was of being given the ruby engagement ring by his grandmother to pass on to the woman he chose to be his bride.

It meant so much to him as some might have thought Joe, as a 'proper' blood member of the family, should have it by rights.

But his grandmother had been firm on the matter.

'Zack, you're the elder and you are to have it. You're the first boy in this generation. That's final.'

'I couldn't have been more unkind if I'd planned it for a year,' Allegra scolded herself. She felt so ashamed.

Ladies Who Lunch

'Sure you'll be all right on your own?' Cathy asked Pete.

She'd got up very early, looking forward to her trip to London.

'Of course. You enjoy your day out with Maeve. I'll have a late supper waiting for when you get back,' Pete reassured her.

'I could pick something up on the way home?'

'Are you suggesting I'm not capable of preparing a simple meal?' Pete asked.

Cathy raised an eyebrow.

'OK, point taken. I'm cooking something simpler today. I e-mailed my tutor and explained about the quiche; she suggested I try to prepare lamb chops and salad.'

'Mmm, sounds nice!'

'I have to photograph the finished meal to show the class on Thursday. We get marks for presentation,' Pete said.

'So you're going to continue with the course?'

'Yes. I feel much more positive about it now. I was reading something by that lady who won 'Bake-off', and she said a good meal doesn't have to take ages to prepare.

'She even suggested some ways to cheat, like using tinned potatoes for a potato salad, that sort of thing.'

Cathy nodded approvingly. The less Pete used the cooker the better, in her opinion, especially when she was out!

If she was indoors she could intervene, as she'd done when he'd cooked the veg last Sunday, but Cathy wouldn't be able to relax looking round an art gallery or flitting through the shops in Oxford Street if she thought her home was about to catch fire.

'I know what you're thinking.' Pete grinned. 'And I'm insulted. I was going to offer you a lift to the train station but I think you can make your own way now!'

'I'd prefer to walk,' Cathy retorted. 'It's a beautiful day and I've plenty of time. I arranged to meet Maeve at the ticket barrier at eight — no need to rush.'

'I was kidding,' Pete said. 'Sure you don't want a lift?'

'Quite sure. Good luck with your homework. See you later.'

'Have a lovely day!'

★ ★ ★

Maeve and Cathy chattered nonstop on the journey.

'How's Allegra getting on?' Maeve boomed. 'What happened when she met up with Zack?'

'She didn't say much,' Cathy replied, keeping her voice as quiet as possible in an attempt to encourage Maeve to do likewise.

Quite a few heads had already swivelled in their direction during the journey, eager to hear what Maeve's views were on the state of the pavements, the bin collections and the government.

Now that the conversation had moved on to family matters, Cathy hoped Maeve would be a little more discreet.

'She said she had an interesting time.

They had pizza. Tiramisu for dessert.'

'Is that all you have to tell me?' Maeve roared. 'I expected something a bit more juicy! Really? No gossip at all?'

Cathy cringed in her seat.

'It's a nice view, isn't it?' she asked. 'Out of the window?'

Maeve stared at the railway embankments covered in scrubby grass and spindly wildflowers. There were piles of misshapen metal pipes strewn about a disused part of the track.

The back walls of neglected terrace houses appeared as they drew closer to the big city.

'Not much of a view,' she said. 'Ah, I get it. Sorry, bit slow on the uptake today. I know I can be too loud.'

Maeve had a voice that could cut glass. It had been very useful in her role as Head of Shelley Primary School, but could be a bit overwhelming at close quarters.

Very soon the two friends were walking through the Turner Galleries in Tate Britain.

'Look at the size of that canvas! It must have taken ages to paint.'

'Mmm, fantastically intense,' Cathy murmured. 'A sensational use of colour.'

'Do you think he was short-sighted?' Maeve asked.

'Short-sighted?'

'The pictures look rather blurry and out of focus — a bit like my vision when I go downstairs to breakfast without remembering to pop my specs on.'

Maeve shrugged.

'I wondered if Turner got the idea of smudging all the colours and edges together because he was short-sighted.'

'I think he was heavily influenced by the French Impressionist painters,' Cathy began.

'Were they short-sighted, too? I suppose they didn't have proper opticians in those days. Aren't we lucky to have been born in this century?'

As soon as they decently could, the two made a bee-line for the sleek and stylish café in the basement and started enjoying pastries and flat whites.

'This croissant is delicious,' Cathy remarked. 'Fresh as can be.'

Maeve's reply was muffled.

'Oh, excuse me, shouldn't talk with my mouth full! I meant yes, scrumptious.'

'Do you remember that school trip we went on,' Maeve said, eyes dancing, 'when Allegra was ten years old. That was when we went to Paris.'

'Do I?' Cathy beamed. 'Such fun!'

'Ladies,' a voice said. 'Sorry to trouble you, but would you mind if I sat myself here, at the corner of your table?'

'There doesn't appear to be any room elsewhere, and . . .'

'Of course, welcome!' Maeve said. 'I'm Maeve and this is my friend, Cathy. I'll budge up a bit, there — all fine.'

'We'll be off in a minute,' Cathy said. 'Nearly finished.'

'Please don't leave on my account. My name is Boris.'

As Boris held out his hand to Cathy, Maeve gave a sudden shriek.

'Are you a singer? Tell me you're a singer!'

119

'Yes, I am, but . . .'

'I knew it! This is similar to what happened last week in one of my TV programmes. My goodness, this is fate, with a vengeance!' Her voice was rising with excitement.

'I'm not quite sure I catch your drift.'

'You're Boris! Boris the bass! The singer!' Maeve's face grew increasingly animated.

'You rescued a whole bunch of musicians last week in Barcelona by stepping in to conduct a rehearsal — you saved the day, without a doubt.'

'Why, thank you,' Boris said, laughing. 'My goodness, I had no idea the story had been so widely reported in the press.'

'I'm Allegra's mother,' Cathy told him. 'We've heard all about you and also your incredible kindness in lending her your violin. We're very grateful.'

'I've heard of coincidence, but this is astonishing!' Boris said. 'In fact, ladies, this calls for another round of pastries.

'Wait until I tell Allegra. She'll be flabbergasted!'

'We know you're taking her to the opera tomorrow,' Maeve told him.

"The Barber Of Seville',' Cathy added.

'My word!' Boris got to his feet. 'You know my life history!'

Once Boris had joined the queue to buy more treats, Maeve leaned forward and spoke in a quieter voice than usual.

'Do you think he's the one? That Allegra will marry?'

A Night at the Opera

'There he is!' Holly shouted. 'Look! Over there!'

Allegra waved frantically to Boris through the throngs of people in Covent Garden foyer, all eagerly anticipating an extraordinary evening's entertainment.

'You both look fabulous!' Boris said, giving both Holly and Allegra an affectionate hug.

'It's so exciting!' Holly squealed. 'A real treat. A box at the opera — you are kind to share this with us, Boris.'

Boris smiled.

'My friend in the chorus managed to get his hands on the tickets for me. He'd like to meet up with us afterwards — is that OK?

'I thought we might all go for a drink, maybe a bite to eat?'

'It would be lovely to meet him,' Allegra said. 'Neither Holly nor I have to be up particularly early tomorrow, do we?'

'One of the best things about being a musician.' Holly chuckled. 'You scarcely ever have to get up early!'

'I'm not sure about that.' Boris pointed to his face. 'See the black rings under my eyes? I'm still suffering from having to get up exceedingly early on Monday.

'I had to be at the station at 6.30 a.m. to catch a train to Yorkshire. I was judging the singing competition at my old school.'

'That sounds fun!' Holly laughed. 'You'll have to tell us all about it, maybe later?'

'Point taken. We need to get to our seats. This way, ladies. And may I say how beautiful you both look this evening?'

'You've scrubbed up pretty well yourself,' Holly said.

'Yes, not bad,' Allegra added.

Boris put his elbows out to the side and Holly and Allegra linked arms with him, ready to join the chattering crowds making their way up the wide expensively carpeted steps.

'Who did you say will be here tonight?'

'Really?'

'Five thousand for one performance?'

'Surely not!'

'But in the papers it said that's the fee he commands nowadays.'

'They'll say anything in the papers. I simply don't believe it.'

'I've no idea who everyone's talking about,' Allegra said, 'But it sounds exciting.'

'Some sort of celebrity?' Holly asked.

'They're exaggerating,' Boris said. 'After all, they're talking about Zack.'

'Zack's here?' Allegra pulled her arm away from Boris.

'Apparently he's been invited to see what he thinks of the production,' Boris said. 'He's made quite a name for himself recently and taking over at the last minute in Barcelona has enhanced his reputation even more.'

'Rumour has it there might be a job opportunity winging its way from the opera house, sooner rather than later.'

'But you're the one who saved the day out in Spain!' Holly said, squeezing Boris tightly to her side. 'Without you we'd all have been completely under-rehearsed.'

'No, Zack's amazing,' Boris said, 'though it's kind of you to flatter me, Holly.

'Now, here we are, our box. We've got it to ourselves tonight so sit in whichever chair you want.'

The three friends pulled chairs right to the front of the box and surveyed the orchestra, picking out faces they knew.

'The double-bass player from Dubai!' Holly said. 'Looks like he's an extra for the evening.'

'And the oboist looks very familiar,' Allegra said. 'I'm sure I've worked with her before.'

Boris started waving madly at some friends of his in the stalls below.

'Wahay!' he yelled and gave them a massive thumbs-up.

Several heads swung round towards the box in a startled fashion.

'Boris!' Holly said. 'Do you have any idea how loud your voice is?'

'Sorry.' Boris bowed his head in mock

repentance. 'I've been asked that many times. Those are old schoolfriends. I haven't seen them in a while.'

'Boris,' Allegra said, 'you don't have to apologise for having a voice capable of carrying across a crowded theatre. Isn't that what you spent years having your voice trained for?'

'Good point.' Boris threw back his head and opened his mouth, as if to test the power of his lungs again, then laughed.

'Don't worry, Holly, I won't embarrass you again!'

'Idiot!' she said, swatting him with her programme.

They're getting on like a house on fire, Allegra thought. They'd make a great couple. I can't believe Holly thought he was keen on me — it's obvious how much he likes her.

Oh, dear, I'm starting to sound like an interfering old match-maker, like Maeve. Although she's almost a match-breaker, as well as match-maker.

Allegra felt ashamed for such mean

thoughts about Maeve and her eyes filled with tears as she reminded herself yet again what a terrible mistake she'd made in breaking things off with Zack.

A tingle ran through the audience as the lights dimmed. In no time, the vast crowd was transported to 18th-century Seville, everyone enchanted by the beautiful melodies, rooting for true love and chortling at the comic turns.

'Aren't you glad you're born in this century, Holly?' Boris asked in the interval. 'You get to choose who you marry, not have your future planned by your guardian, being given away to the highest bidder like our poor heroine.'

'Absolutely!' Holly's eyes sparkled with anger. 'The way woman were treated, it's, well, words fail me.'

'It's a story,' Boris reminded her.

'And there's a happy ending coming up,' Allegra added. 'At least, I think there is, if my memory isn't playing tricks.'

'Oh, yes,' Boris said. 'Quite a complicated plot, pretty ludicrous.'

'Aren't they all?' Allegra countered.

'Quite!' Boris agreed. 'Ah, bang on time,' he continued as there was a knock at the door. 'Here's our refreshment. Ladies, take a glass, if you please.'

'Champagne?' Holly shrieked. 'Boris! You are divine. What have we done to be spoiled like this?'

'Just your wonderful self,' Boris murmured, 'I mean, yourselves,' he added, turning to include Allegra.

'My mother and Maeve are still raving about what a gentleman you are,' Allegra said, a smile on her lips.

'Of course! It was an absolute pleasure to see them at the Tate. Who'd have thought it? Such a coincidence!'

'Almost like an opera plot,' Holly added. 'I haven't spotted Zack, by the way. Have either of you?'

'No.' Allegra's voice was small and tight.

'No sign of him.' Boris frowned. 'He was supposed to be here. At least, that's what everyone was saying before.'

'What happens next, Boris?' Holly asked. 'In the opera, I mean.'

'Ah, you're going to love the second half,' Boris said. 'It begins with the hero disguised as a singing teacher — pretty close to my heart, this bit. It's hysterical, too, you wait and see.'

The second act passed in a delightful jumble of comedy, farce, heavenly music and poignant emotion until at last, after all the intrigue and innuendo, love flourished as it should.

As the curtain went down for the last time, Allegra realised they had been mistaken.

Zack was in the audience, right down in the stalls, at the end of the front row. She hadn't noticed him at first.

He was wearing a dinner jacket and had his hair neatly combed back, his curls for once tamed to polished perfection.

Next to him was a woman with shoulder-length wavy hair. Zack had her hand clasped in his.

The clapping intensified as the soloists took their curtain calls.

'Thank you, Boris,' Holly said. 'What

a great evening!'

'Yes,' Allegra echoed. 'You're so thoughtful and kind.'

Boris put his arms round Holly and Allegra, hugging them both affectionately. He gave Holly a peck on the cheek.

Allegra fixed her gaze on Zack again and as fate would have it, he turned to look up and their eyes locked across the vast amphitheatre.

Allegra felt her heart beat more loudly than the drums had in the opera performance. How could no one hear?

The sound was echoing, echoing round the auditorium. Da dum, da dum, da dum, faster and faster.

'I mustn't leave you out, Allegra,' Boris said, the champagne flowing freely in his veins.

He reached over to give her a kiss on the cheek.

Zack scowled as he looked up at the trio; he turned back to his neighbour in the seat beside him and whispered something in her ear.

Not again! Allegra thought, her cheeks

flaming scarlet.

Zack had seen her kiss Boris in the restaurant in Spain, then he'd noticed Boris hug her on the plane and hadn't seemed to be happy about that.

And now he'd seen Boris kiss her. What must he think? If he minded, which he seemed to, did this mean he still had feelings for her?

But if he did, why didn't he mention them the other night when they had had a meal together?

More to the point, who was his mysterious companion?

Parks and Palaces

'Thank you, Boris, but I've a bit of a headache. You go on with Holly and have a meal together. Thanks so much for a lovely evening.'

'If you're sure? I don't like the thought of abandoning you like this,' Boris said. 'Will you be all right getting home?'

'Of course.'

Allegra smiled encouragingly at Boris and Holly. She didn't see why they should have to change their plans because she wasn't feeling too well.

Her head had started throbbing when Zack had turned to look at her in the opera house and all she wanted to do was go home and lie down. It didn't mean the others shouldn't enjoy themselves.

'I could come back with you,' Holly offered. 'I don't like to think of you travelling by yourself. It isn't right.'

'Honestly, it's nothing,' Allegra insisted. 'I'm overtired. I've had a great evening but I'm happy to go home now. Besides, you two will enjoy being alone together.'

She winked at Holly, who blushed furiously.

'Shame my friend, the tenor, wasn't able to join us,' Boris said, 'but I can catch up with him another time.

'He's decided he should have an early night as he's got to be up at the crack of dawn to catch a plane to France.

'His agent called this evening saying there was an opportunity due to a soloist being ill. Would he like to sing in 'Messiah'? Lucky him! I'd jump at a chance like that.'

'A bit like when Zack was able to conduct at short notice, to help out when Rostopovsky was ill,' Holly said.

'Indeed!' Boris turned to Allegra. 'Let us at least walk you to the Tube. It's on our way — I insist.'

'Thank you,' Allegra said.

The three friends made a winding passage through the crowds to the underground station and, with many more apologies and lashings of sympathy, Boris and Holly went on their way.

Allegra pulled her jacket around her as she made her way down to the platform, choosing to take the stairs. She wasn't fond of lifts and thought the exercise might help to clear her head.

Not that there was much fresh air down here, she realised as she breathed in the thick, stale atmosphere.

The platform was thronged with people, many clutching opera programmes and talking excitedly about the thrilling evening they'd had.

As Holly boarded the train she spied an empty seat and made a bee-line for it, only to find an elderly gentleman nearby.

'Please, have this seat,' she said, indicating the vacant space.

'Thank you, my dear.'

'Allegra! Here, take my seat.'

It was a voice Allegra hadn't expected to hear this evening. A voice she heard all the time in her head, belonging to the person she was head over heels in love with.

'Thank you,' she whispered and sat down gratefully.

'Not with your friends?' Zack asked.

'Boris and Holly have gone out for a meal but I'm not feeling a hundred per cent, so I'm on my way home.'

'Boris should have taken you home.'

'I can manage.'

Zack's eyes burned into her.

'A gentleman would take his girlfriend home,' he insisted.

'He's not my boyfriend. I don't know why you should think he is. He's actually very fond of Holly, as is she of him.

'Not that there's anything settled between them; they haven't know each other long, but I think I know Holly well enough . . .'

'Are you match-making?' Zack asked.

'No!' Allegra smiled. 'I really do have a headache, but I also know they won't mind being left together. That's a bonus, and stops me feeling guilty because I know I haven't ruined their evening.

'In fact, I've probably made it better for them. Another friend of Boris was meant to be joining us, but he cried off at the last minute. A work commitment.'

'Had Boris set you up with a blind date?' Zack asked.

Allegra looked at him. She wondered why he was being a little possessive, for want of a better word.

'I don't think it was a blind date,' she replied. 'I think it would have been four friends out for a meal after a lovely evening at the opera.'

Zack stared out of the window, clenching and unclenching his fist.

'I presume you're going to Victoria?'

'Yes. And you?'

'Still in the same flat in Clapham,' Zack said. 'So, yes.'

Should she ask him about the woman he was with, Allegra wondered. It was none of her business, but he'd been asking her all sorts of questions.

'Did you enjoy the performance?' she asked instead.

'I did.'

'I heard you might be working at Covent Garden soon.'

'Who told you that?' Zack asked.

'I think it was Boris. Some other

people were saying things, too — members of the audience.'

'It's a possibility,' Zack said. 'We shall see.'

'It sounds a very exciting possibility,' Allegra enthused. 'Congratulations! It's a real feather in your cap.'

Zack broke into a smile, making his whole face light up.

'I'd forgotten how enthusiastic you were about everything, and how generous you are with your praise.

'How's the headache, by the way?'

'Lifting.' Allegra stood up. 'We need to change here to another Tube line.'

By the time they reached Victoria her headache had completely disappeared. They made their way to the gigantic notice board in front of the platforms and looked for the Brighton Line for trains to Clapham and Croydon.

'Oh, no!' Allegra said in dismay. 'There's a delay. It'll be at least forty minutes.'

'It's usually such a good service,' Zack said. 'I wonder what could be wrong?'

'It'll be a leaf on the line or something quite trivial.'

Allegra sighed and tucked her hair behind her ear.

'You should go home by a different route, Zack. Lots of trains go through Clapham. Don't let me hold you up.'

'I've a better idea,' Zack said. 'We could go for a walk. It's not far to St James's Park.'

'It's a long way,' Allegra said, 'and it's quite late. Will St James's be open? Surely the city parks don't stay open at night?'

'There's one way to find out,' Zack said, a huge grin on his handsome face, the corners of his mouth curling up attractively.

'Tell you what,' Allegra suggested, 'I reckon we've got time to walk to Buckingham Palace, right on the edge of the park, before we have to turn round and come back for our train. I'm up for it, if you are.'

'Race you!' Zack shouted.

As she hared along the streets with

Zack, Allegra felt happier than she had for a long time.

She was glad she hadn't asked him about the woman he'd been with at the opera. Hadn't Boris said Zack had been invited to attend the performance because he might be offered some conducting there?

The woman was probably part of the management of the opera house. Or she might be his agent. Something similar.

But he had been holding her hand at one point, Allegra remembered, feeling uneasy. However, she reasoned, Boris had given her a kiss and that hadn't meant anything except friendship.

Allegra frowned a little as she tried to square the idea of a professional partnership, with a job offer looming, with holding someone's hand. She failed.

I'll ask him, she thought. When the time is right. If I feel brave enough.

Very soon the pair arrived in front of the floodlit palace. Allegra gazed up at the monumental building, home to some of the most famous characters in British history over the last couple of hundred years or so.

'It's so romantic!' Allegra clasped her hands together. 'I can imagine the young Queen Victoria inside, with her beloved Prince Albert. Such a tragedy he died young.'

'You should live in a palace.'

Zack was closer to her, so close she could breathe in the tangy citrus smell of his aftershave. Old memories flooded her senses and she began to tremble.

Allegra turned to face him, the tension between them unbearable.

As he bent his head down she closed her eyes for a second, then stepped back in alarm, frightened of what might happen next.

Determined to break the mood, she spoke brightly.

'You think I should live in a palace? Are you suggesting the lovely flat I share with Holly is anything less than a palace?'

Zack looked down at the gravel.

'I meant . . .' he began as Allegra,

gathering her courage, continued.

'Do you mind my asking, who was the lady you were with this evening? At the opera?'

'Someone very dear to me,' Zack said softly. 'Someone I haven't known long, yet I feel as if I've known her for ever. I hope she'll always be part of my life.'

Allegra was silent as she contemplated the enormity of what Zack was saying.

I had no right to ask him, she thought. I have no claim to him. What nearly happened between us just now, the kiss that never was, means nothing.

I threw my chance of happiness away when I chucked the ring at him. This serves me right.

Of course he's met someone else. Why wouldn't he? Talented, good-looking, famous and successful, too. No doubt he has women from all the corners of the world pursuing him!

'Sorry, text. I have to look at this,' Zack said, getting his phone out of his pocket.

Allegra knew it was from the woman when she saw Zack's perfect face soften and crease into a smile as he read the message.

'I'm glad you're happy,' she said stiffly. 'My goodness, I think we have to get back — our train will be arriving shortly.'

Zack looked up from his phone, one eyebrow raised.

'Ah. I see what you're thinking, Allegra. Yes, the text is from the lady at the opera. She's everything to me because I've been looking for her for so long.

'It's like a new life — I can hardly explain it.'

'Who is she?' Allegra asked, light dawning.

'She's my mother.'

Love Finds a Way

'His mother? Allegra, what on earth are you talking about?'

Cathy sat down at the kitchen table, perplexed as she chatted to her daughter on the phone on Thursday morning.

'Why is it unusual for Zack to have seen his mother? Or to get a text from her?'

'Mum, let me explain.'

'His mother's such a nice lady. Remember when we all went out for a lovely lunch, shortly before you got engaged?' Cathy went on. 'Your father and I clicked straight away with both of Zack's parents.

'And, of course, I got to know her pretty well when we worked together to arrange your engagement party . . .'

'Mum!' Allegra interrupted.

'Yes?'

'Please listen. There's something you don't know. I couldn't tell you before, because Zack didn't want me to, but he doesn't mind people knowing now.'

'Ah,' Cathy said. 'I thought there was something.

'His mother once said to me she was sure Zack would share his story with us at some point. I wondered at the time what she meant. So, what is the big secret?'

Cathy blinked as all sorts of explanations thronged into her mind, to be rejected.

If Maeve had been listening, Cathy mused, she would have come up with all sorts of possibilities: a secret first disastrous marriage like Mr Rochester in 'Jane Eyre'; maybe a spell in a Young Offenders' Institute after an unfortunate mistake in his youth.

Maeve found it hard to separate normal life from fantasy — Cathy was not going to make the same mistake.

'The big secret is, Mum, Zack was adopted as a baby.'

'Is that all? Sorry, I don't mean to make light of the situation. Of course, it must be a big thing to deal with.

'Is Joe adopted? No, I see. Explains

why the two brothers look different. It had never occurred to me to wonder why before.

'And you say Joe's engaged now?'

'Yes, to Vanessa,' Allegra said.

'Vanessa, what a lovely name. Anyway, carry on with telling me about Zack. Your father and I had no idea he'd been adopted.'

'He didn't tell me until after we became engaged,' Allegra said. 'He found it very difficult to talk about and I think it made him anxious for the future, about having a family of his own.'

'Oh, Allegra, I wish you'd told me all this. Such a thing for Zack to face, and for you.'

'He didn't want me to say anything at the time,' Allegra said, 'so I couldn't.'

'You've always been loyal and good at keeping confidences, but I can see how challenging it must have been. I'm pleased he doesn't mind you talking about it now.'

'I knew you'd understand, Mum.'

'Allegra,' Cathy began. 'Tell me to

mind my own business, but was this anything to do with why you and Zack split up?'

There was a long silence from the other end of the phone.

'Sorry, darling,' Cathy said. 'I shouldn't have asked.'

'It had something to do with it,' Allegra said eventually, 'but we split up mostly because I wasn't able to offer Zack the support he needed.'

Cathy spent some time talking to her daughter, reassuring her and trying to comfort her.

'In the end,' Cathy said to Pete once the call was ended, 'I told her how much we loved her and said that I thought she'd done the best she could at the time.

'We none of us find it easy to cope with the big issues in life and it sounds as if she and Zack were overwhelmed with the enormity of his situation.'

'None of it sounds a walk in the park,' Pete agreed. 'But I have to say, love, if they couldn't cope, perhaps they weren't meant to be together.'

'I disagree,' Cathy said softly. 'I think they are perfect for each other and it's one of the things I feel saddest about.

'Allegra met the love of her life and it was all going swimmingly but somehow she managed to let him slip through her fingers. Or perhaps circumstances conspired against them.'

'You could be right, but we shouldn't interfere,' Pete reminded Cathy.

'I know, but it's tempting,' she said. 'What I wouldn't give to put the two of them in the same room together and force them to talk to each other honestly.

'I'm sure they'd be able to sort things out.'

'It's been a whole year since they split up. A lot of water under the bridge.'

'You're probably right.' Cathy sighed. 'They're not the same people they were. I know Allegra's changed since they split up.'

'And we don't even know about Zack,' Pete continued, 'not having seen him for a long time. He's a big name in the classical music world.

'Does Allegra even know if Zack is attached? A man like that, with the world at his feet . . .'

'Allegra says he's not with anyone else,' Cathy said.

Pete scratched his head.

'What about the meal they had on Monday? Why did Zack want to meet up with Allegra?'

'Apparently it was Zack's mother's idea — his birth mother, I mean. Allegra says he had told her all about being engaged and how it had ended abruptly.

'She advised him to meet up again properly with Allegra, after having met her unexpectedly on tour which had been awkward for both of them, initially at least.

'She said he should have a good chat with Allegra and make sure they could be friends, particularly as they were bound to work together again in the future, now that his career's taken off.'

'It sounds sensible,' Pete said. 'It can't have been easy for either of them to suddenly see each other in Barcelona after having split up last year.

'If they're friends they won't have to dread running across each other again, will they?'

'It may sound sensible,' Cathy said, 'but I'm not sure it's true. Not if, as I suspect, Allegra is still in love with Zack. Oh, why are affairs of the heart always complicated?'

'Love will find its way through paths where wolves fear to prey,' Pete quoted.

'What? Pete!' Cathy could scarcely believe her ears. He was still able to surprise her.

'Lord Byron.' Pete cleared his throat. 'He knew a thing or two about love.

'One of my favourite quotes; I tended to trot it out in the 'A' level English lessons when I was teaching.'

'I see. And the relevance? Despite it being a desperately romantic saying, I'm not sure it applies in this situation. What do wolves have to do with anything?'

'I mean,' Pete said, 'that we don't need to worry unduly. If Zack and Allegra are meant to be friends, well, if they are friends again now — no problem.

'If there's meant to be more ahead for them, then love will find its way, even if the path is a difficult one such as fierce creatures like wolves would be scared to take.'

'You think our job is to stand back and let love get on with it.'

Pete put his arms round Cathy.

'Yes. You certainly don't need to worry about it — not as much as you do, anyway.'

'But worrying is part of my job description,' Cathy said.

Pete planted a tender kiss on his wife's cheek and picked up the apron from the hook on the back of the kitchen door.

'I need to make haste,' he said. 'I'll see you anon, after my cookery lesson. Let's hope the tutor sets an easier homework this week.'

'Indeed.' An image of the burned quiche flashed into Cathy's mind.

'I know what you're thinking,' Pete said with a chuckle. 'What have you got planned for the day? Is it the charity shop, or one of your reading ladies?

'I can't keep up with all your good works.'

'Volunteer library delivery for Mrs Oatcake — she got through the books I took round last week very quickly and is desperate for more — then yoga class, to cope with the stress of my life.

'After that, I'm having coffee with Maeve before we do a charity shop shift together.'

'Yoga!' Pete beamed with pleasure. 'That gives me a chance to tell you one of my jokes. I've been saving this one up.'

Cathy groaned.

'No! Please!'

'When you get to your yoga class, make sure to do the Worrier Pose.' Pete sniggered. 'Get it? Not Warrior Pose, but Worrier. Your favourite.'

'I got it.' Cathy sniffed. 'I just didn't think it was funny.'

'No offence meant, my darling. Besides, I know you're not really offended because you're trying hard not to smile, but failing miserably.'

Cathy shook her head.

'See you later. Don't bother about supper because I'll bring something back from cookery class; we're making hotpot today.'

The phone rang as soon as the front door had clicked shut behind him.

'Hello? Mum, I've got some exciting news!'

'Hi, Allegra. Is it about Zack? Are you and he . . . ?'

'No, nothing like that. It's to do with one of my pupils, Cassie. Her father is a policeman, high up in the Met.

'He's been taking an interest in my missing violin and he rang me a few minutes ago to say that, at last, it's been found!'

Lost and Found

Allegra hurried to the police station to collect her violin, almost tripping over her feet in her haste to be reunited with the instrument.

'Thank you! I'm so grateful — oh, how disappointing. I'm afraid this isn't mine.'

Allegra looked at the cheap case the policeman had in front of him on the table and struggled to hold back the tears.

'Wait a minute before you decide,' the policeman said. 'Take a good look inside the case.'

She did so.

'Oh, how wonderful! Yes, officer, thank you. It is my violin, but in a different case.'

'It's common for a thief to change the case,' the policeman advised. 'Some cases have tracker devices in.'

'I didn't have anything like that.'

The policeman smiled.

'It looks unharmed. Those scratches and marks are all old, aren't they?'

'Yes. The result of being played for . . . let's see, the violin was made in the late 1880s. So probably over a hundred and thirty years.'

Allegra cradled her violin protectively; she'd missed it so much. She reached into the case.

'I still have my lovely bow, too. I'm glad the thief kept it with the violin. The instrument isn't complete without it.'

'We think the criminal definitely knew what he or she was doing,' the policeman said. 'You were probably targeted as you left the rehearsal.

'They were after a valuable violin and bow, the sort used by a top professional.'

'What do you think happened to the case? It wasn't anything special, but if it turns up, I'd be pleased to have it back.'

'Of course,' the policeman said, 'although it's unlikely it will reappear. It was probably discarded or sold on right after the instrument was stolen.'

'I understand, officer. I'm really grateful to have the violin and bow back — the case and other contents are replaceable.'

Except for my favourite snaps, Allegra thought sadly. The ones of Zack and me at the seaside, taken in the photo booth.

Those ones where we're happy and in love, before life got complicated.

★ ★ ★

After repeating her thanks, Allegra set off to East Croydon Station to catch the train up to London. She had an orchestral rehearsal that afternoon at the Albert Hall followed by a concert in the evening.

She was carrying two violin cases. One contained her own dear violin, from which she had already vowed she would never be parted again. The other was Boris's.

Allegra leaped on to the train as the doors were closing and spotted someone.

'Holly! Great. I was hoping we'd be catching the same train.'

155

'You got your violin back!' Holly beamed. 'Oh, Allegra, I'm so happy for you. Did they tell you about how it had been found?'

'It was because of something Boris said. You know, about posting on various musical sites about the violin having been stolen, with photos.'

'He knows so much about music and everything, doesn't he?' Holly said. 'He is an amazing sort of guy.'

Allegra smiled.

'You're completely smitten, aren't you? I think he feels the same.'

Holly blushed.

'How can you be sure?'

'I noticed how very attentive he was towards you at the opera. And when you came home yesterday after your meal you couldn't stop talking about him.'

'I was amazed you were still up when I got home — I thought you would have gone straight to bed with your headache.'

'It got much better. My train was delayed for quite a long time.'

'Why do I get the feeling, just like last

night, that there's something you're not telling me?'

'You're very imaginative?'

Holly folded her arms.

'Intuitive, not imaginative.'

'All right,' Allegra said. 'There is something, but you'll have to wait. I'm too excited about my violin.

'You wanted to know how it was found. Because of Boris's excellent advice, the auction houses were on the alert for a stolen violin.

'Sure enough, my violin was offered to a famous auction house in Paris, you know the one, very high prices, always in the news.

'Anyway, the police were tipped off, and a man was arrested when he came to deliver the violin and bow to the auction rooms, mistakenly thinking he was about to get away with selling a stolen instrument.

'After his arrest he quickly spilled the beans about how he got the instrument and the police traced the trail back to the original thief, who pleaded guilty straight away.'

'Wow!' Holly gasped. 'Your violin has certainly travelled about a bit since leaving the restaurant.'

'Yes,' Allegra said, 'but luckily it's been carefully looked after.'

'The thieves would have been stupid not to keep it safe, considering its value,' Holly remarked.

'True.'

Allegra patted the case on her lap.

'I need to get it checked over to make sure, but it looks fine to me. I can't wait to start playing it again.'

She looked at the other violin case she had brought with her, wedged between her knees and resting on her feet.

'I had to bring Boris's violin with me because I couldn't be sure my own violin would be in a fit state to play.

'I'll try to get it back to him as soon as possible; he must have been missing playing it.'

Holly's face bore a soppy expression on hearing Boris's name mentioned.

'On the other hand,' Allegra said,

'maybe he has found a new interest.'

Holly leaned forward.

'I haven't forgotten,' she said.

'Forgotten what?'

'I'm still waiting; you promised to tell me what happened after we left you at Covent Garden Tube.'

'Oh, that.' Allegra peered out of the window. 'Look! Nearly at Victoria. Time to get off.'

'Allegra!' Holly said. 'You promised.'

'It's nothing,' Allegra said. 'I happened to meet Zack.

'We travelled to Victoria and went for a walk, right up to Buckingham Palace, as the trains were all delayed.'

'You went for a late-night walk with Zack. What happened?'

'Thank goodness the trains run all night back to Croydon — we're lucky to live where we do,' Allegra said.

'You're doing it again,' Holly insisted.

'Doing what?'

'Talking about something else in order to avoid talking about Zack. Come on — what's the news?'

'We need to get out,' Allegra said. 'Come on.'

As the two friends scurried along to the underground, juggling with three violins between them plus bags which contained their concert clothes, Allegra turned to Holly.

'He won't mind if I tell you about his secret. You remember I said there was something I couldn't tell you about him because it would be breaking a confidence?'

'Oh, yes,' Holly said. 'It sounded so mysterious.'

'It's not a mystery or a secret now,' Allegra said. 'It's all out in the open. I was talking to my mum about it this morning on the phone.'

The girls had reached the barriers to get on to the Tube line and both fell silent as they negotiated their way with their instruments and bags through the narrow opening, tapping their Oyster cards.

'I'll fill you in later,' Allegra said. 'It'll take time to tell you his story and it will be best if it's somewhere private.

'You should know Zack's much happier. Everything's going to be fine for him now. But there's no hope.'

'No hope?' Holly echoed. 'What do you mean?'

'No hope of us getting back together,' Allegra said. 'No hope at all.'

'Don't Give Up'

Every time she saw the Albert Hall Allegra felt her spirits lift and today was no exception.

The massive bulbous, casserole-like shape stood proudly at the top of the flights of shallow stone steps, welcoming Holly and Allegra as they joined a throng of orchestral players who were making their way from Prince Consort Road up to the mighty building.

Walking round the giant structure to the Artists' Entrance, Allegra thought of all the times she'd performed there before, starting with when she was a teenager in the National Youth Orchestra.

'Do you remember when we first met?' she asked Holly.

'I certainly do. It was my first orchestral course with the Youth Orchestra and I didn't know a soul. You were so friendly — made me feel at home right away.'

Allegra smiled.

'You were the same. Both of us new-bies together, at the back of the second violins.'

'It can be so scary going away from home for the first time.'

'Don't I know it!' Allegra said. 'And that archaic school where we stayed and rehearsed — it was like something out of Harry Potter.'

'I think Harry Potter might actually have been filmed there, if I'm not mis-taken.'

'I think you're right. But the highlight of the course was performing here at the Albert Hall,' Allegra said.

'Absolutely!' Holly replied. 'And here we are again.'

The two friends hurried in through the entrance and made their way downstairs to the backstage area. In no time at all they were seated on the vast wide stage, waiting for the conductor to arrive.

'I'm meeting Boris between the rehearsal and the concert,' Holly whis-pered to Allegra. 'He's on his way to an audition but has suggested we meet in Hyde Park for half an hour or so. Do you want to join us?'

'I'd love to,' Allegra said, 'as long as I won't be in the way. I don't want to be a gooseberry.'

'Don't be silly. Boris always likes to see you.'

'I can give him back his violin,' Allegra said. 'It seems a good opportunity. He has been so kind, letting me borrow it all this time.'

'He is exceptionally kind,' Holly said.

'He's quite the most —'

'Shh,' the leader of the orchestra said. 'The conductor's on his way. Let's tune, ladies and gentlemen, shall we?'

The oboist played her A and, section by section, the musicians carefully tuned their instruments.

A percussion player decided to join in the fun by pretending to tune the triangle, much to everyone's amusement.

★ ★ ★

In the break, Holly and Allegra made their way to Hyde Park. The statue of Prince Albert regarded them from his memorial as they crossed the busy road.

'Looks fabulous, doesn't he?' Allegra said. 'After his restoration and refurbishment. Look at the gilt.'

Holly screeched with laughter.

'I thought you were talking about Boris to begin with,' she said. 'Look, he's there, waiting for us. He certainly looks fabulous, but I'm not sure he's been restored or refurbished!'

'Or has anything to be guilty about,' Allegra quipped.

'What are you two laughing at?' Boris asked as he greeted them warmly. 'And what's this? My violin! Don't tell me they've found yours at last?

'I'm thrilled! I hope they've caught the thief.'

'It seems half the police in Europe have been involved in tracking Allegra's instrument,' Holly told him. 'Interpol has been busy.'

'Yes, they've caught the thief,' Allegra

explained, 'and quite a few of the middle men. Thank you, Boris. I don't know what I've have done out there in Spain if it hadn't been for your generosity.'

'Someone would have come up with a violin for you to borrow, no doubt.'

'But it wouldn't have been as good as yours,' Allegra replied. 'I'm very grateful. Thank you.'

'My pleasure,' Boris said. 'I'll do anything for one of Holly's friends.'

With that he linked his arm through Holly's and the three of them set off across the grass, marvelling at the warmth of the September day and how the summer was lingering longer than usual.

There were a few crunchy leaves beginning to fall on to the green carpet of grass, but generally speaking it was as if summer was still in full swing.

'I saw another article about Zack in the paper,' Boris said. 'What a hero he was for saving the day in Spain and how he has a glittering career ahead of him.

'There is some talk of him going out to Sydney. He's been offered some conducting dates over there in Oz.'

'A great career opportunity,' Holly said.

'How are things working out for you, Boris?' Allegra asked. 'Anything exciting in the pipeline?'

'As a matter of fact, there is,' Boris replied. 'You remember I went up to my old school, to judge the singing competition? It turns out one of the kids' parents is a big noise in the musical theatre world.

'He heard me give a quick demonstration in the competition when I was adjudicating, and on the strength of that he's asked me to audition for the main part in a big show he's putting on next year!'

'Phenomenal!' Holly squeezed Boris's arm.

'I'm off to meet up with him now,' Boris said, 'which means, I'm afraid, it's time to leave you two ladies. I'll ring you soon, Holly. Bye, Allegra.'

Boris strode off in the direction of the nearest bus stop, his violin bouncing along as he carried it on his back.

Allegra and Holly continued their walk in companionable silence until Holly turned.

'You look fed up.'

'Sorry! I'm trying not to inflict my mood on you,' Allegra answered.

'You can inflict your mood on me as much as you want,' Holly said, 'if you think it will do any good. But it's not the answer, is it?

'Why don't you tell me what happened? We've still got a bit of time before we have to be back. Here, let's sit down on the bench. Enjoy the sun while we can.'

'All right. But I don't know where to begin.'

'What was the last thing Zack said to you?' Holly suggested. 'We can start there.'

'He said he was seriously thinking of accepting.'

'Mysterious!' Holly smiled. 'Now you'd better tell me the back story. I can't help if I don't know the facts. Besides, you said he didn't mind if you talked about it, because it isn't a secret any more.'

Allegra settled on the bench and told Holly all about Zack's adoption. How he'd decided, once they were engaged, that he wanted to find out who his birth parents were, or at least trace his mother.

'He'd always been happy in his adoptive family and that made it difficult at first. He didn't know how his adoptive parents would react if he wanted to find his mother, although they'd always reassured him they would be there to support him, come what may.

'They had always thought the day would come when he wanted to know — needed to know — exactly where he came from, and would want to meet his mother.'

'How tricky for them all and how sensible his parents sound,' Holly said. 'Go on. What happened next?'

'I'm not sure,' Allegra said. 'His need to find his mother created a lot of tension between us, my lack of understanding and immaturity made it all much worse and we split up. My fault.'

'It doesn't sound as if it was anyone's fault, Allegra. It was a difficult and stressful time; you were both faced with a situation you couldn't control or cope with.'

'Thank you for not blaming me,' Allegra whispered.

'You've blamed yourself enough,' Holly said. 'Let's think forwards now, not backwards. What can be done?'

'Nothing at all. Zack's made that clear. Now he's found his mother, he wants to spend as much time as possible with her.'

'But it doesn't mean he can't rekindle his romance with you.' Holly frowned.

'Yes, it does.' Allegra bit her lip. 'You see, he wants so much to be a part of her life that he's willing to change his.'

'Change his life? In what way?'

'He's thinking of giving up all the regular work he has in Europe and moving to live near his mother, maybe even with her, in the States, in Washington.

'She married an American and has a family out there. Zack has a half-brother and two half-sisters and he wants to be with them. They're all he thinks about.'

'But his future!' Holly cried. 'What about the chance to conduct at Covent Garden? Surely he wouldn't throw a career opportunity away?

'And Boris mentioned something about Australia.'

'He doesn't care about fame and fortune, he said. There's a job going at the American University in Washington, a sudden vacancy due to illness. He's already been interviewed over Skype and they offered it to him straight away.

'It's for one term initially, but can be extended to a permanent post. It's not his usual thing, more of an academic post with some conducting; it would be a big change.

'He needs to decide very soon if he's going to accept it.'

Allegra lifted her hand to her mouth, then pulled it away as she realised she was about to bite one of her nails. She hadn't done that since she was eight years old.

She needed to pull herself together.

'What about you?' Holly asked. 'Doesn't he care about you?'

'There's no room for me in his life.' Allegra shrugged.

'Did he say that? In those exact words?'

'Not exactly.' Allegra was thoughtful. 'He said we'd had something special, but it hadn't stood the test of time. The first difficulty that popped up, we crumbled.

'He didn't blame me. He blames himself for being secretive and not allowing me to support him through the situation. But I don't think he sees any future for us.'

'He's making the same mistake again,' Holly protested. 'He's not asking you to wait and he's pushing you away instead of letting you help.'

'I think Zack doesn't feel about me the way he used to. He said he hoped I'd meet someone better suited than he'd been.

'He said he was surprised I hadn't already met someone else by now — he thought that I must have lots of men interested in me.'

'Did you make it clear how you felt?' Holly urged. 'Did you tell him he was the man for you?'

'No, I couldn't. It wouldn't have been fair to burden him with my feelings.'

'So Zack has no idea how you feel. And when you told me he was seriously thinking of accepting, you meant he might be about to put a hold on his career to go and live in Washington with his mother and her family, with no immediate plans to return to this country. Do I have that straight?'

Holly put her hand up to the sky.

'And, to top it all off, I think I felt a drop of rain. As if things couldn't get any worse!'

'That's about it,' Allegra replied. 'The new term at the American University starts early next week.

'If Zack accepts the job, I have to forget him.'

The heavens opened at this point with one of those sudden autumn storms.

As the two girls ran back to the Royal

Albert Hall, passing Queen Victoria's beloved husband again on his high plinth, Holly shouted to her friend.

'Don't give up, Allegra — please don't give up!'

Worthless Books

'Sciatica? Oh, Maeve, poor you. I'll be round as soon as I can. Bye!'

Cathy put her phone down and scribbled yet another task on her list of the day.

Maeve needs help with housework.

'Let me see.' Pete looked over Cathy's shoulder.

Go to library, collect more books for Mrs Oatcake and deliver.

'How can one woman read so many books?' he questioned.

'She doesn't read all the ones I pick,' Cathy explained. 'I'm not too good at it, to be honest; I always seem to get it wrong.'

'Mmm.' Pete grunted. 'I suspect it may be a clever ruse to get you back sooner rather than later. Mrs Oatcake is just wanting the company.'

'Maybe.' Cathy's hand trembled as she held the list. 'But I'm still being useful, even if that is the reason.'

'You're overtired,' Pete said. 'Have you had breakfast yet?'

'Haven't had time,' Cathy mumbled. 'I've been up for ages.'

'I'm making some toast now.'

Pete grabbed the loaf from the bread-bin and started hacking into it.

'Doctor's orders.'

'I always enjoy your toast,' Cathy confessed. 'And the hotpot you brought back yesterday from class was delicious.'

'Glad you liked it.'

'I'm looking forward to the meal tonight. What are you cooking? What was homework this week?'

Pete curled his lip.

'The tutor said maybe to try something like macaroni cheese, something simple. I wasn't the only person in the class who'd had a disaster with the quiche last week.

'She wondered if she'd been a bit over-enthusiastic, expecting us to cope something quite advanced, so this week we're all making a pasta dish.

'She recommended macaroni cheese

for me, but some of the others are allowed to make lasagne.'

'Lasagne's quite complicated,' Cathy said. 'Maybe not impossible,' she added hastily after looking at Pete's downcast expression, 'but certainly time consuming.'

'You wouldn't want to spend all day in the kitchen, would you?'

'No, but I don't like being fobbed off with macaroni cheese, either. I might try lasagne.'

'Have another look at my list,' Cathy said, hoping to distract him. 'Ah, yes. Next item.'

Cover Maeve's shift at the charity shop.

'You do too many shifts already,' Pete counselled. 'I've mentioned this before but you haven't taken a blind bit of notice. And what's this? 'Collect autumn plants from garden centre'.'

'The garden's looking a bit scruffy,' Cathy argued. 'It could do with some autumn colour.'

'We could do that together at the weekend?' Pete suggested.

'OK,' Cathy said, crossing it off the list.

Ironing.

'There's not much ironing, is there?' Pete asked.

'There's a mountain to tackle!' Cathy replied. 'It's almost filling the spare room now.'

'Does it matter?'

'Yes, because Allegra will be staying for a few days next week. She has a concert coming up in Bristol and she's bringing Holly with her.

'I need to get both the rooms ready for their visit.'

'Listen, I'll do the ironing after I get back from cooking,' Pete told her. 'You know how I like to iron while I watch a film on my tablet.'

Cathy nodded gratefully. Secretly she was finding life overwhelming.

Having looked forward to her retirement for years, she was finding she didn't seem to have as much time to herself as she'd thought she would.

Instead, an endless procession of

chores and duties seemed to appear each morning as she tried to decide how to spend her day.

* * *

Mrs Oatcake was all smiles when Cathy arrived at her door. 'Come in, come in,' she said. 'Coffee's made and there's shortbread.'

Cathy politely took a piece of shortbread and perched on the edge of the sofa in Mrs Oatcake's front room.

'I've been looking forward to your visit all morning,' Mrs Oatcake declared. 'Now, let's discuss books.'

'I hope you had fun with the historical novels I chose for you last time,' Cathy began a little timidly. 'I was worried, though, that perhaps the one about Henry the Eighth and his second wife might have been a little too bloodthirsty.

'Old Henry did seem to go in for beheadings with monotonous regularity!'

'They were all right.' Mrs Oatcake

curled her lip. 'Not very adventurous, though. Not even the Tudor one. Not much violence.

'Don't you realise my favourite television programme is 'Game Of Thrones'?'

Cathy blinked.

'To be honest,' Mrs Oatcake continued, 'I feel you were still palming me off with some tame stories. I do hope you weren't judging me, thinking at my age I couldn't take the strong stuff?'

'Of course not!' Cathy said in shocked tones. 'I would never patronise you.'

She pulled a couple of books out of her bag to show Mrs Oatcake.

'I did wonder about these,' she said, offering two books the librarian had recommended Cathy take for Mrs Oatcake.

'All the other ladies who have the home volunteer visits seem to love them.'

'They're rather different from my previous choices,' Cathy said. 'I asked the librarian for help, but in fact, now I look at them properly, I'm not sure they're suitable . . .'

'Aha!' Mrs Oatcake almost snatched the books from Cathy's hands in her haste to scan the covers. 'Worthless books! Exactly what I've been hoping you'd bring me.'

'Worthless books? Oh, I'm sorry.'

Cathy felt flustered and embarrassed. How could she have got it so wrong again?

Yet Mrs Oatcake's face was alight with happiness. What had she meant by 'worthless'?

'Worthless books,' Mrs Oatcake repeated. 'We were never allowed to read these at school — well, not often. Mostly, we weren't allowed to finish them.'

'And you want to read them now? Cathy's eyebrows shot up so high they nearly disappeared into her fluffy thick hair.

'Of course! It'll be one in the eye for the nuns. Not that they'd mind at all. It was all pretence, a sort of double bluff.'

'I think you'd better give me a bit more explanation,' Cathy begged. 'I'm feeling a mite confused.'

'I'll fetch some more coffee,' Mrs Oat-cake said. 'This might take some time. Back in a minute.'

Cathy looked round the sitting room while Mrs Oatcake was in the kitchen, wrestling with the new-fangled coffee-machine she'd shown Cathy on a prior visit.

Meanwhile, Cathy admired the family photos in their silver frames, the orna-ments brought back from all corners of the globe and the impressive chess set that had belonged to Mrs Oatcake's dear departed husband.

'Drat!' Cathy could hear from the kitchen, followed by 'Double drat!'

She knew from experience not to rush to help Mrs Oatcake. The coffee-machine was Mrs Oatcake's pride and joy, bought for her by her son for her birthday.

If she was left alone with it, she would eventually remember how to tame the mighty beast into submission and would return to the front room bearing two deliciously strong coffees — coffees that would be the envy of many of the fancy outlets in town.

Whoever thought older ladies preferred weak tea was very much mistaken, in Cathy's opinion.

'Here we are, dear.'

Mrs Oatcake appeared at the door with a precariously balanced tray, staggered to the table and set it down with a bump.

'Hot and strong — like my men.'

Cathy looked a little shocked to hear this, but Mrs Oatcake winked and waved her hand graciously as if to bat away any possible offence.

'Something we used to say at school, my dear,' she explained. 'Completely meaningless, but we thought we were very grown up saying it and it had the advantage of annoying the nuns; our main aim in life, of course.

'Now, where were we? Ah, yes. School. You know I went to a convent boarding-school in the 1940s?'

'No, I didn't.'

Cathy settled back in her seat. She

had time, as Pete had crossed off the garden centre visit from her list and he was going to do the ironing, too.

'Well, I did.' Mrs Oatcake looked into the distance.

'I'm sorry,' Cathy said. 'How terrible to be parted from your family.'

Mrs Oatcake cackled.

'Nonsense, we had a whale of a time. Of course we missed our parents, but there was a war on and so many children were away from their families that we never felt sorry for ourselves.

'We spent the whole time haring around the school, larking about. I didn't learn much — not from the lessons, such as they were — but it didn't seem to matter.

'Anyway, we had a good school library, well, reasonable by the standards of the time. I'm sure the nearby boys' school had a much better one, but that's another story.

'The point is, at the weekend we were allowed to read what the nuns called 'worthless books'. They were the recently published, contemporary, thrilling books, full of murder and romance.

'Terribly tame, I'm sure, if you compared them with modern books, but we loved them. Once the weekend was over, though, we had to return them whether we'd finished them or not.

'During the week we were only allowed to read so-called 'improving' books, mostly the classics and biographies of the Saints. Quite a dull collection, truth be told!'

Cathy's eyes were out on stalks. She'd never heard anything like this before.

At least when Pete had confiscated books at school he had returned them at the end of the day.

'It must have been so frustrating,' Cathy commiserated, 'to be halfway through a book, especially an exciting, plot-driven book, and not to be allowed to continue with it until the next weekend.'

'It was. We all learned to speed read but, even so, you invariably tended to be halfway through a really cracking read when you were forced to return it.

'And there was always the danger it wouldn't be available the next weekend,' Mrs Oatcake continued. 'We suspected the nuns were reading them themselves, and why shouldn't they? But we never had any definite proof.

'There was one time when my friend decide to go and snoop in the nuns' quarters to see if she could find a particular book she was wild for . . . But I digress.

'It became part of our vocabulary that any up-to-the-minute books, books we actually wanted to read, were referred to as 'worthless'.

'The worthless books I'm hoping to read now are the recently published books, the ones everybody's reading. The exciting, up-to-the-minute ones.

'I don't want you to censor what I read because I'm advanced in years! I still feel the same inside, just as I've always done.

'Besides, my friend's coming to stay soon and she reads very widely. I'd like to have the chance to discuss worthless books with her.'

'I see. So you think these books I've brought today are OK?'

'Absolutely!'

'I was beginning to wonder,' Cathy confessed, 'and please don't take this the wrong way, but there was something my husband suggested. He's often wrong, I hasten to say!'

Mrs Oatcake roared with laughter.

'You're about to tell me you thought I was being a little over-fussy about the books I wanted because I was lonely, aren't you?

'That's a very common misconception among the volunteer library helpers, or so my friends all say.

'No, I was hoping you'd start bringing me some up-to-date reads, ones with guts, telling it how it is.

'I want to read about modern life, warts and all.'

Cathy laughed.

'I'm sorry I got it wrong.'

'It's my fault — I should have been more specific. I apologise.

'I suppose I didn't want you to think badly of me, realising I wasn't interested in those pesky biographies and worthy tomes you've been dragging here.

'I knew we'd get there in the end.'

Cathy grinned at Mrs Oatcake and tapped the bright shiny covers of the recently released, wildly successful blockbusters in front of her on the table.

'I tell you what, when you've finished with these two beauties I'll have a go at reading them myself!'

Mystery Benefactor

'My mum says she's hardly ever in the kitchen these days,' Allegra told Holly.

The two girls were chopping salad in the tiny galley kitchen in their flat. Leaves occasionally blew against the window, flung up by a chilly October breeze.

Holly put her head on one side.

'I thought your dad was, how can I put it? Struggling a little with the culinary arts?'

'You mean he's a useless cook?'

'Yes!'

'He was, but Mum says he's getting really good now. Taking it all very seriously, of course. He keeps suggesting they need to buy all sorts of gadgets like a pasta maker, juicer, that sort of thing.'

'Ah, yes. To be used once, then stored, cluttering up the kitchen cupboards.'

'Exactly,' Allegra said.

'Still, at least you know what to give him for Christmas.'

'Holly! How could you?'

'What?'

'Mention Christmas. It's only October.'

'I've seen Christmas cards for sale.' Holly sliced the end off a cucumber. 'And I heard one of your pupils playing 'Jingle Bells'.'

'Fair cop.' Allegra grabbed a spring onion and peeled back the thin outer layer. 'And I'm flattered.'

Holly's eyes twinkled.

'You mean because I recognised the tune?'

'Yes! Cassie is getting much better at the violin now,' Allegra said.

'Her dad was kind, wasn't he?' Holly remarked. 'To take a personal interest in finding out about your violin.'

'Yes, he was. And your Boris was magnificent, helping out in all sorts of ways in Barcelona.

'I rather miss his violin. I must ask him to bring it round next time he visits you. He can play to us.'

Holly ripped open a bag of salad leaves and scattered them into a bowl.

'He'd like that. He'll be round later in the week. I've asked him over for supper.'

Allegra gave Holly a sidelong glance.

'You're growing very fond of him, aren't you?'

'More than fond,' Holly muttered. 'I've never felt quite like this about anyone before.

'I'm not sure I trust my feelings, though. It's all been so quick.'

'He feels the same?' Allegra asked gently.

'He says he does. Oh, Allegra, I think I'll burst if I don't tell you. I think I'm falling in love with him.'

'You didn't have to tell me.' Allegra drizzled dressing over their salad.

'Oh, I'm sorry!' Holly stuttered. 'I didn't think. Sorry, Allegra. I didn't mean to hurt your feelings.

'How tactless of me, after all the upset you've gone through with Zack!'

'No, silly!' Allegra laughed. 'I meant you didn't have to tell me you're falling in love with him, because I already knew!

'It's written all over your face every time you talk about him and I'm totally convinced he's the right person for you. No doubt about it.'

'Phew.' Holly sighed. 'I'm relieved. I thought I'd put my foot in it.'

'Not at all. Let's eat. The lasagne should be ready.'

Allegra pulled a supermarket lasagne out from the oven and plonked it on to the table next to the salad.

'Apparently my dad has mastered homemade lasagne now!'

'Impressive!' Holly gave a thumbs up.

'Yes. He made a massive batch of it — Mum had to freeze some. We might get to sample it next week when we're down there.'

'It's kind of your parents to let me stay.'

'You're more than welcome,' Allegra replied. 'They've plenty of room now it's just the two of them at home.'

'Nevertheless, it's a lot of work to have house guests, even if we will be out most of the time, over in Bristol.'

'I'm looking forward to the concert in

St George's,' Allegra said. 'It should be great fun.

'I thought we could go down on Monday afternoon and spend the evening with my parents. We won't have to get up too early to be in Bristol for the rehearsal on Tuesday morning.'

'That sounds perfect,' Holly said as she crunched into a piece of celery. 'A bit like this salad.'

'I forget to tell you,' Allegra said as she passed Holly the garlic bread. 'The police contacted me again to say my violin case has turned up at last.

'The contents have been taken, as we suspected they would have been, but the case is still in good shape.'

'That's good news,' Holly said.

'Yes. It doesn't matter about the spare bow — it wasn't worth much — or the strings. All are replaceable, except . . .'

Holly raised an eyebrow.

'Except what?'

Allegra fiddled with the salad bowl.

'I had two photos tucked deep inside the case, under the lining. I'm sorry to have lost them.'

'Did the police say they weren't there?'

'They said the case was completely empty.'

'Photos of Zack?' Holly guessed.

'Yes.' Allegra's eyes glittered.

She was not going to cry, she thought. Not over photos.

Holly put her hand on Allegra's shoulder and let it rest there lightly for a minute or two until Allegra recovered.

'One day, when we went to Brighton, we had some of those photos taken in a seaside booth. You know the sort of place,' Allegra explained.

Holly nodded.

'There were four photos in a strip, all nearly identical. Just of the two of us. We each kept two photos; I kept mine in my violin case.'

'Where is the case?' Holly asked. 'Do you have to collect it?'

'That's the funny thing,' Allegra said. 'The police said the case had been sent over from Spain directly to someone else who was looking after it on my behalf.

'It was one of my friends, apparently, and he's going to bring it round. He told the police he wanted to give me a surprise.'

'It must be that policeman,' Holly said. 'You know, your pupil Cassie's dad.'

'I thought it must be him at first, too,' Allegra said, 'but the police said no, it was a musician friend who'd been out in Spain with me when the violin had been stolen.'

'They said they don't usually bother with a stolen case because it isn't that valuable.'

'I understand what they mean.' Holly chewed thoughtfully. 'The police have enough to do without chasing after violin cases. And at least they found the actual instrument.'

'Exactly.'

'But who is this mystery person?' Holly queried. 'It's all sounding a bit elusive.'

'Yes! The Scarlet Pimpernel?'

'Johnny English, more like!'

Allegra forked up a helping of salad. 'Mmm, I love radishes. Anyway, I'll know soon enough, because they'll bring it round.

'Oh, Holly, do you think it could be Zack? He hasn't let me know about his job offer, the one in Washington.

'I know he said he was seriously thinking of accepting it, but he hasn't been in touch to say he's going.

'I'm starting to hope no news is good news and he's decided not to take it.'

'I'm sure he wouldn't leave without contacting you,' Holly said, 'not now you're friends again. It wouldn't be fair.'

'Friends don't emigrate without saying anything,' Allegra agreed, 'and he said he wanted us to be friends again. We are friends again.'

Holly leaped up as the doorbell went.

'Are you expecting a pupil?' she asked.

'No,' Allegra said. 'You?'

Holly shook her head.

'Maybe it's the mysterious violin-case rescuer?'

Holly ran downstairs to the front door and shrieked when she saw who the visitor was.

'Boris! Come in. We weren't expecting you, but what a lovely surprise!'

'I've something for Allegra,' he said, holding her missing property aloft.

'Come on up,' Holly said. 'Allegra will be pleased to see her case again!'

'Hello, Boris!' Allegra said as he stepped into the tiny hall of their top-floor flat. 'How kind of you to bring my case round. Have you eaten?'

'I have, but I could easily eat some more, if you're offering.' Boris plonked himself down at the table. 'I expect you're wondering how I've got your case?'

'The police told me it had been found and a friend would be bringing it here.

'You are very kind, Boris, to take a personal interest in returning it.'

Boris ran his hand through his hair.

'It wasn't quite like that . . .' he began.

'I'm thrilled!' Allegra interrupted, almost snatching the case from Boris. 'I just need to check something.'

She pushed her fingers down inside the lining of the case, all the way round, and even tugged at a loose part of the velvet cloth to look underneath, but in vain. There were no photos.

'Should there be something in there?' Boris asked. 'You're searching quite thoroughly.'

'Wait.' Holly pointed at the velvet. 'Look! There's something stuck underneath. See?'

Allegra squealed with joy.

'My photos!' she said, lifting them to her lips and kissing them.

'What in the world?' Boris scratched his head.

They were indeed her photos, looking a little the worse for wear, slightly more dog-eared and faded, but still the treasured reminder of happier days.

She stuffed them back into the case, suddenly embarrassed at her display of emotion.

Holly whispered something to Boris and the puzzled expression left his face.

'Ah, none of my business, but I think I get it now.' A frown appeared again. 'However, I think you might have got the wrong end of the stick.'

Allegra looked at him, her emotions under control for the time being, at least.

She couldn't wait to be alone in her room with her photos, to have another look at them.

Besides, something was bothering her. She couldn't put her finger on it. She needed to have another look at those photos as soon as she could.

'What does that mean, Boris?' she asked as she sat down at the table again.

Boris helped himself to a massive portion of pasta and three slices of garlic bread. He smiled at her.

'That means I do hope you don't think I'm the one who's been chasing your case and arranging for it to turn up here tonight.

'No, the credit has to go to someone else entirely.'

Allegra's fork stopped in front of her mouth before she had a chance to taste the lasagne and she swallowed, her mouth dry and uncomfortable.

Her heart fluttered. Could it be? Could Zack be her mystery detective and saviour of the case?

Boris coughed.

'I don't know if you were aware of this, Allegra, but when we were out in Barcelona Zack was the one who collaborated with the local police and kept on at them every day, berating them for not finding your violin.

'He was like a man possessed, determined you should have your instrument back, come what may.'

Allegra's hand flew to her mouth.

'I had no idea.'

'He went round to the local market every day, convinced your case might turn up on a bric-à-brac stall even though the violin was long gone. If the case turned up, maybe it would have some clues like fingerprints.

'He befriended all the stallholders, explaining what had happened to you and giving them his mobile number so that they could contact him if they saw or heard anything.'

'Good gracious!' Holly sat back on her chair. 'What happened next, Boris?

How was it found?'

'Zack's hunch was correct,' Boris continued. 'A young lad, who regularly scavenges the streets for junk and offers it to stallholders to earn money for his family, found Allegra's case.

'The thief probably discarded it pretty quickly to throw the police off the scent, as a case tends to have personal stuff in. Yours even has your initials engraved on the leather handle, Allegra — a bit of a giveaway.

'Anyway, the case was found by this lad a couple of days ago, long after the violin had been recovered from the auction. It was discarded down by the river, sheltered by some trees.

'The contents had been stripped out — except for your photos, obviously, which were extremely well hidden — and the boy took the case to the stallholder, thinking it might have some second-hand value.

'It had been out in all weathers so there was no chance of fingerprints or other clues. But no-one needed more evidence because the violin had already been found and the thief had pleaded guilty. You might even call it an open-and-shut case!'

'Boris!' Holly groaned. 'That's terrible.'

'I hope the boy trying to sell the case didn't get into any trouble,' Allegra said.

'Yes,' Holly agreed, 'that wouldn't have been fair. He wasn't the thief; he was only trying to raise a bit of money.'

Allegra nodded.

'Not everyone's as lucky as we are.'

'Anyway,' Boris said, 'it seems Zack had thought of everything. He'd asked the stallholders to report the case to the police if it was found. He had also left money for the stallholders to buy the case if it was offered to them, plus enough to send it back to England, to his address in Clapham.

'No doubt he wanted to surprise you one day by bringing it here.'

'Impressive,' Holly said.

'Zack was always good at planning,' Allegra said dreamily. 'You have to be, to conduct an orchestra.'

'And so,' Boris chipped in, 'the case was sent to Zack. He's the one you should be thanking because, without him, you wouldn't have got your case back — or the violin, come to that.'

'But Boris,' Holly said, 'you played a massive part in getting the violin back.

'You were the one who recommended putting out information on those websites, to alert the musical community to the fact Allegra's violin had been stolen and might possibly be offered for sale.'

'I'd love to take the credit,' Boris said, 'but again, it was all down to Zack. I passed on the information to you — he asked me to and to leave his name out of it.

'He didn't want to take any of the glory but I don't see why I shouldn't tell you now.

'So I was only partly 'instrumental' in getting your property back. Get it? Instrumental?' He roared.

Holly chuckled to hear further evidence of Boris's wit.

'I owe Zack so much,' Allegra said, her face scarlet. 'Why didn't he want me to know he was helping?'

'Perhaps,' Holly suggested, 'he thought that if he offered you the advice you might not accept it, not after . . .'

Allegra nodded sadly.

'Tell you what,' Holly said. 'Let's have some pudding. Cheesecake or apple crumble?'

'Would it be rude to have both?' Boris licked his lips.

Holly swatted him on the shoulder.

'You greedy thing!' she said. 'Of course it would be rude, but when has that ever stopped you?'

Holly brought the puddings over to the table and Allegra cut into the cheese-cake first.

'Here you are, Boris,' Holly said, passing him a laden plate. 'But there's one thing left I don't understand.

'Why did you end up bringing the case here? Not that it isn't lovely to see you, of course.'

'Yes,' Allegra echoed. 'Why?'

Boris waved his hand to indicate he'd love to talk but currently had his mouth full and, as a polite, well-brought up member of society, he had no choice but to wait a little longer before speaking.

'Ah, an easy question,' he managed to say a minute or so later. 'Zack asked me to bring the violin case round to you on his behalf. I'm his postman, if you like.'

'But why?'

Allegra frowned. Was it because he couldn't face her? Or could he not be bothered?

He had said they were friends — surely he could have popped in with the case? She would have liked to have thanked him for all his efforts.

Why did he have to be secretive? Again!

With a growing sense of horror, Allegra realised she probably already knew the answer to her question.

She knew why Zack hadn't come here, tonight. That he was, in fact, unable to come.

Boris halted the progress of an enormous spoonful of cheesecake on its way to his mouth and confirmed her worst fear.

'Zack couldn't come round because he's on his way to America.'

Back to School

'There's so much to do!' Cathy complained to Pete.

'Why not write one of your lists? I know it's a busy day, with Allegra and Holly arriving this evening, but we can get through the chores together.'

Cathy sat down and started scribbling:
Clean whole house.
Food shopping and cook casserole.
Garden centre.
Shift at charity shop.
Vacuum Maeve's carpets.
Go to library to pick up next lot of books for Mrs Oatcake — deliver.
Church flowers.

'The whole house doesn't need cleaning — kitchen, bathroom and a quick tidy will do,' Pete said. 'You know Allegra and Holly won't notice. We've seen their flat!'

'Still, the food shopping needs done; you can't say that's not necessary.'

'I'll do that,' Pete said. 'And I'll cook

the casserole for this evening. You look doubtful. It's hotpot under another name, isn't it? And you said my hotpot was fine.'

'If I run out of time there's still plenty of lasagne in the freezer.'

'So there is. And your hotpot was delicious. Ditto the lasagne.' Cathy smiled.

Maybe her list wasn't as overwhelming as she'd thought. Pete was getting on brilliantly with his cooking now and she'd noticed he did better if she stayed out of his way and let him make decisions.

At last, he was settling down into his retirement.

'The garden centre, why?' he mused.

'We never got round to picking up a few plants at the weekend, did we? I don't want to cross it off the list, as it was on the last one, if you see what I mean.'

'I do, but there is such a thing as being a slave to the list. It's an aid, not a dictator.'

'Don't exaggerate, Pete.'

'If I've told you once, I've told you a

million times that I never exaggerate! Sorry, Cathy. The garden centre's a good idea, though. Do you know why?'

'Yes. The café does lovely coffee.'

'Spot on. And pastries, don't forget the pastries. What's more, they sell those cakes that can be passed off as home-made.'

'Yes! Super idea.'

'Do you remember when you used to have to make cakes for Allegra when she was at school?'

'Do I? I couldn't keep up with the constant demand from the Parents' Association to send in home baking.

'They never seemed to consider that people had jobs and didn't want to spend every evening baking for charity sales, even if it was to raise some cash for the school.

'And all the parents of the children in Allegra's class knew full well I taught at the same school.'

'They were a pretty demanding bunch,' Pete agreed, 'But you made some good friends there, too.'

'I do miss all that,' Cathy said, 'and I miss my colleagues.'

'Anyway, back to the cakes. We used to be able to make cakes look home-made, didn't we?' Pete said.

'Buy a shop cake, take it out of the packet, bash it round a bit . . .'

'. . .and pop some extra icing sugar on,' Pete finished. 'Fooled them every time!

'I told my cookery class that story and they all thought it was hilarious. What's more, many of them admitted they'd done the same sort of thing.'

Cathy looked at the list again.

'All the remaining chores are for other people,' she noted. 'The church, Maeve, Mrs Oatcake.'

Pete grimaced.

'Yes, and what's more, you ran the vacuum cleaner over Maeve's carpets a few days ago. Why would they need doing again? Has she been having wild parties?'

'She has much higher standards than we do,' Cathy explained. 'Besides, I didn't manage the whole house; there simply wasn't time.

'I couldn't do the sitting-room properly, because Maeve was in there watching her soap and it would have been painful for her to move.'

Pete ran his hands through what was left of his hair.

'I bet she was scoffing chocolates, too!' he exploded.

'How did you know?'

'Experience.'

'Oh, Pete, it doesn't matter. Please calm down. You know I like to be useful.'

After a few deep breaths, Pete sighed

'Cathy, maybe you're doing a little too much for other people. I didn't like to say so, but you've been looking tired and run down this autumn — though, of course, as lovely as ever.

Cathy fiddled with a button.

'I've been worried about Allegra,' she admitted. 'But, yes, I agree. I am doing too much and feel a bit dragged down by it.'

'I know you've been keen for me to start enjoying my retirement,' Pete said, 'and I think I am now, eventually. In fact, I'm having the time of my life at cookery class! 'Bake-off' is my new favourite programme and I've made a lot of new friends.

'I thought I'd have some of them round soon, maybe next week, for Sunday lunch. Don't worry; you won't have to lift a finger.'

'That sounds lovely, and I am enjoying my retirement, too,' Cathy said, 'but I miss teaching.

'I'd prefer to be helping kids to learn their alphabet to arranging the church flowers any day, but I don't want to let people down.

'It's all my own fault — I took on too many responsibilities as soon as I gave up work. The opposite of what everyone advised.'

Pete picked up his mobile.

'Leave it with me,' he said. 'You go and get ready to be whisked away to the garden centre. See what I did there? Whisked? Cooking is that close to my heart now!'

Cathy groaned and went up to her bedroom. She couldn't do anything about Pete's terrible sense of humour, but perhaps she could do something to her hair before the outing to the garden centre.

She wondered if they would have some of those gorgeous autumnal scarlet and mustard blooms. The ones that supposedly provided colour throughout the transition between summer and winter. Or had she left it too late?

Cathy grabbed a bottle of a potion which promised to tame her locks and gave her crowning glory a good squirt.

Mmm, she thought. Not bad. At least it had got rid of the worst of the 'first Mrs Rochester' look.

Now for some lipstick. Better, much better. A blast of perfume and she was ready to go.

'Why are you looking secretive?' she asked Pete as she joined him in the hall.

'I made a few calls,' Pete said. 'You're off the hook for the rest of the day.'

'You can't go cancelling my commitments without asking!' Cathy was horrified. 'People depend on me. Pete, this is wrong — I feel guilty.'

'I'll tell you all about it once we get going.' Pete opened the door and gestured to Cathy to go first. 'If I had a cloak, I'd throw it down for you to walk upon,' he announced. 'As it is, you'll have to dodge the puddles and run to the car.'

* * *

'This place gets more and more like a village, not a garden centre.' Cathy marvelled at the displays of plants, books, kitchen equipment, even clothes.

Plus, of course, the impressive array of garden furniture.

'Can we look at the sheds?' Pete asked, 'I like a good snoop around the sheds and outbuildings.'

'If you think we've got time.'

'We have, my love. Remember I've cleared your duties for the day; well, nearly all of them.'

'You still haven't said how.'

'I rang the church flower-rota lady and explained you had visitors coming this evening and were up to your eyes in chores.

'She said it wouldn't be a problem as they have the Brownies coming in to help today; she was adamant that you weren't to worry about it.

'Next, I rang the charity shop. They were equally understanding and said you wouldn't be missed. Ah, that came out wrong. I didn't mean they wouldn't miss you, but they said they'd manage.

'Then, as I was about to ring Maeve, she rang us.'

'I thought I heard the house phone.'

'She doesn't need you to do her carpets any more. She said she's been feeling as if she's been taking you for granted for a long time now.'

'Is her sciatica better?'

'No, but she's invested — her word, not mine — in one of those new robotic vacuum cleaners. She's having the time of her life watching it whizz round the house.

'Admittedly it doesn't do the stairs, but it's fantastic on a level surface, she told me. It sounds as if she's practically wearing the carpets out; it's having to work very hard.

'She said we can borrow the appliance whenever we want and suggested this afternoon. What do you think?'

'How kind. Dear Maeve, what a smashing idea. And Mrs Oatcake?'

'Ah, Mrs Oatcake.' Pete fell silent for a moment. 'She's a character, isn't she?'

'One way to describe her.'

'I rang her,' Pete explained, 'but she refused to countenance the idea that you might not be coming round to see her.

'She said you needn't bring any more books, as she's still reading the last lot, but she wants to discuss them with you and would be very upset not to see you today.

'She told me to say she has short-bread.'

'Shortbread?' Cathy said. 'Then I'm sure I can spare the time to visit for tea. Thank you, Pete, for helping me out. I don't know what I'd do without you.'

The two of them spent a happy 10 minutes wandering in and out of the outdoor building display, housed in a sunny corner of the garden centre.

There were gazebos and garden rooms as well as more traditional sheds. Cathy sat on a chair inside an office pod and looked at the space where a computer would go.

'This reminds me of my little office corner in my classroom. Oh, I do miss teaching,' she said.

'Your phone's ringing.'

'Thanks, I didn't notice. Hello? Head-master! Yes, this is Cathy. Yes, it has been a long time.

'You'd like me to what? When? Of course. I can be there in half an hour. See you soon!'

'What's going on?' Pete asked.

'They want me back!' Cathy said excitedly. 'Just for a few hours, the rest of today. A teacher has been injured at Shelley Primary — they snapped their Achilles tendon.'

'Ouch!'

'The new Head's asked me if I would possibly be free to go in and lend a hand. It's the Reception Class and they can't cover with the staff who are already there — they've more than enough work to do.

'He rang me first before he rang the agency for a supply teacher, on the off-chance I could go in.'

'Let's go,' Pete said. 'What are we waiting for? I'll have you home in a jiffy to collect anything you need, and then run you down to the school.

'How does that sound?'

★ ★ ★

In no time at all Cathy was sitting with the Reception class. She gazed at the bright, eager faces in front of her, all turned in her direction like a host of sunflowers seeking out the light.

'Now, children, what have you brought to show everyone? We're going to have a lovely display on the nature table.

'Don't be shy; who wants to start?'

She smiled at her class while they all put their hands up, even those who had forgotten to bring anything to show.

Several children looked as if they might burst with the effort of not calling out.

'Well, that is lovely! I am so pleased with you all. Let's take it in turns to bring our objects up and put them on the table.

'Here's the first one. A dark red leaf. What a lovely colour! Did anyone else bring leaves? Let's have a look at them. Good.

'Conkers next. I can see we have a beautiful selection waiting to be shown.'

Great quantities of shiny conkers of various sizes were released on to the table and a few immediately skittered off the hard surface and bounced across the floor, much to everyone's amusement.

One little boy held out his hand to Cathy, slowly releasing his fingers one by one, like a petal unfurling, to reveal his surprise.

'Goodness me! I know magpies are supposed to like bright shiny objects — did you find this in a nest?' Cathy asked.

'Course not. It was in me mum's joolery box. I looked in and found this yellow ring with shiny bits stuck in it.

'Do you like it? I fort it was nicer than a conker or a leaf.'

'I like it very much, but I might put it in this envelope from my desk. Here, I'll stick the flap down and pop the envelope back in the drawer, then I can telephone your mum at lunchtime to let her know her ring is safe at school.

'She can pick it up from me later when she collects you.'

Cathy smothered a smile. She was having so much fun!

'Let's move over to the rug by the board,' she said. 'If you can sit down cross-legged, we'll have a little chat about all the interesting objects you've brought in. Is everyone comfortable?'

'I don't like sittin' cross-legged, miss. Hurts me legs.'

'Put your legs to one side, then. Super! Now, first I'm going to choose an item from the table and whoever brought it in can tell us all about it. What have we here?

'A photo of a field with a beautiful row of trees at the end and some digging, yes, quite a lot of digging. Who brought this in?

'Well done. It's a great photo and shows lots of tree roots and a big pipe, too. There's a fence around it — it looks like a building site. Where is it? Oh, I know. That big area they're developing.

'And this is what it looked like yesterday? What a fascinating photo, and a worthy addition to the nature table. In all my years of teaching, I have to say I don't ever remember anyone bringing in such an interesting photo before.

'Your brother took it for you on his phone? And printed it off for you to bring into school? How kind of him.'

'Miss, did they have photos when you started teaching?'

'Yes, they certainly did,' Cathy said,

'but it was much trickier to get the pictures printed out.

'Yes, there were colour photos, not
only black and white. Things were different in 'the olden days', but not quite
as different as you might imagine!'

In her lunch break, when the children
were playing outside, Cathy took the
chance to photograph the nature table.

She thought she would show the photos to Mrs Oatcake when she nipped in
for tea on her way home.

★ ★ ★

'Here it is,' Cathy said. 'The nature table
in all its glory.'

'We used to have a nature table.' Mrs
Oatcake nodded. 'But we didn't bring in
photos for it.'

'Yes, that was a new one for me,' Cathy
admitted.

'Wait a minute,' Mrs Oatcake said,
frowning. 'What's that weird thing, sticking out of the mud? Show me the photo
again.

'A little bit nearer, please. Can you enlarge it? More? That metal object looks familiar.'

'It just looks like an old pipe to me,' Cathy said, 'like something from a farm machine.'

'No. I've seen one of those before, when I was a child. That's not a pipe. It's an unexploded bomb, left over from the war!

'You need to report it, Cathy, right now. It could be very dangerous.'

Danger Ahead

'Why are the roads closed? There can't be flooding, can there?' Allegra stopped the car.

'There hasn't been enough rain,' Holly said. 'It's funny — the satnav is telling us to go straight on but the road is closed.'

The friends were on the outskirts of Bath on their way to stay with Cathy and Pete.

'There's a bomb!' a stationery motorist ahead shouted. 'We have to wait until it's defused.'

Holly wound down her window.

'Sorry,' she said. 'I couldn't quite hear you. I thought you said there was a bomb.'

'I did! Turn on your radio. We've made the national news! Have to wait here until it's sorted, I guess.'

Holly waved her thanks, closed the car window and switched on the radio.

'An unexploded bomb has been found on a building site just outside Bath, in the West

of England. Precautionary measures have been put in place.

'There are road closures and home owners in the immediate vicinity have been asked to leave their homes and go to nearby community centres ...'

'A bomb?' Holly said. 'There can't be a bomb, not here in the West Country!'

Allegra switched the car engine off.

'Good thing I've some biscuits,' she said. 'We could be here a while.'

'Boris has texted,' Holly said. 'He wants to come down to see if I'm all right. What a sweetie. I'll tell him there's no need.'

'Will they even be running trains down to Bath?' Allegra asked.

'The station's nowhere near the evacuation area,' Holly answered, studying her phone closely. 'I'll read what it says here, on the BBC news site.

'Don't worry, Allegra. Your parents will be fine. Everyone will be fine. It's a precaution.'

Allegra's phone got a text from Pete.

No problem here, love. We're both safe.

You might have some trouble getting into Bath, but take your time.

Your mother discovered the bomb! Long story. Call you when I can.

'I need to tell you something,' Allegra said.

'I knew it!' Holly spun round in her seat to face Allegra. 'You've been so quiet since Saturday evening, when Boris came round to dinner.

'It's something about the violin case, isn't it? Something's upset you.'

'Yes and no. It's not the case. It's the photos.'

'The ones hidden under the lining? But I thought you were ecstatic to have got them back again?' Holly said.

'I was. I am. But when I found them, they didn't look right.' Allegra rubbed her eyes.

'What do you mean, they didn't look right?'

'They were the wrong way round.'

'The wrong way round?'

'Ae you going to repeat everything I say?' Allegra asked in exasperation.

'No.'

'I'll start at the beginning of the story — that will be easiest.'

'Yes, it would! Because what you're saying isn't making a whole heap of sense at the moment.'

Holly sat back in her seat and let out a long breath.

'We've plenty of time.' Allegra said. 'By the look of the traffic building up I've no doubt we'll be stuck here for ages.'

'Spit it out,' Holly demanded. 'But no crying. I can't bear to see you unhappy.

'Let's make a deal. If you feel like crying, you have to eat another biscuit. OK?'

'OK. I'm going back to the day Zack and I visited Brighton. Oh, no, I already feel like having a biscuit!' Allegra reached for the custard creams.

'Munch away, and get on with the story — I'm dying of curiosity here.

'I'll have a biscuit, too. No, I don't feel like crying. I feel like a biscuit.'

'You don't look like one.'

'Allegra! Concentrate on your story. Please.'

'We had a fantastic time in Brighton,' Allegra said. 'Spent the whole day larking about on the beach, chasing seagulls, eating ice-creams and making plans for the future.

'Before we went home we spotted one of those seaside photo booths, the ones where you put coins in a slot and they take four photos in rapid succession while you sit there. We thought it would be fun to have a record of our perfect day.'

Holly handed Allegra another biscuit.

'Thanks,' she muttered. 'We squashed together on the little stool — it was a tight squeeze — and posed, remaining as still as we could. Then we waited outside for the photos to drop out of the machine.

'You know how you're supposed to wait a few minutes for the photos to dry before you handle them? I couldn't wait; I took them out when they were still a bit tacky and put my thumb right in the middle of the set of four, so there was a slight smudge on the two middle photos in the strip.

'Zack carefully tore the set of photos — he kept the top two photos and I had the other two.'

'And you kept your photos in your violin case — and now you have them back,' Holly supplied.

'No, I haven't.'

'What do you mean?' Holly asked. 'I saw them. You've got your photos back.

'Wait, do you mean . . . ?'

'Yes. My photos were the bottom two photos and had the torn strip at the top, with the top photo smudged from my thumb.

'The photos in the case have the torn strip at the bottom, with a smudge on the lower picture. And the pictures are very slightly different, the sort of differences you'd only notice if you'd been studying them for years.'

'So you think Zack kept his photos, too, and swapped them over! Do you need a biscuit?'

'No!' Allegra's eyes were shining with excitement. 'Don't you see what this means, Holly? If he kept his photos all this time, maybe it was because they still meant something to him. As my set of photos meant something to me.'

'The big question is,' Holly said, 'did he swap them over by mistake?'

'Possibly.' Allegra sat motionless in her seat.

'Or was it on purpose?' Holly said. 'To send you some sort of message?'

The motorist behind Allegra's car gave a sudden beep and a friendly wave, trying to attract her attention to the fact that the traffic was moving again.

'And we're off,' Allegra said. 'Talk about this later?'

In 20 minutes the two friends reached Cathy and Pete's house. As they pulled up outside Allegra's father rushed out to greet them.

'Thank goodness!' he exclaimed. 'It's all over at last; they've defused the bomb.

'Your mother's quite shaken. I had to go and collect her from Mrs Oatcake's house.'

'Who's Mrs Oatcake?' Allegra asked as she hugged her dad.

'I forgot you didn't know her,' Pete said. 'Hello, Holly! Lovely to see you. Come in, both of you.

'Mrs Oatcake's here, too. She refused to be left out, and Maeve's here, as well. It's quite a party.

'Like the war spirit, Mrs Oatcake says. She's been telling us stories from her childhood about bombs and wartime.

'Apparently her father was a doctor in Birmingham during the war. He was given the George Medal by the King for his heroic deeds. Even Maeve is impressed.'

Very soon, Holly and Allegra were sitting down with Pete, Cathy, Maeve and Mrs Oatcake.

'Tell us more about it, Mum!' Allegra begged. 'The whole story, from beginning to end.'

Cathy did so.

'And the best news,' she concluded, 'is that the headmaster rang a little while ago. He's offered me a job, part-time, just two afternoons a week, but it's what I want.'

'I thought you'd retired,' Holly said.

'Yes, but it's complicated,' Cathy began.

'Cathy wasn't enjoying retirement as much as she thought she would,' Pete said. 'She missed teaching too much.'

'This is the perfect solution,' Maeve chipped in. 'You'll have time for the charity shop.'

'And your volunteer reading,' Mrs Oatcake added.

'While having time with the kids at school,' Cathy agreed.

'And still having time to yourself,' Pete added in a stern voice, his gaze lingering on Maeve and Mrs Oatcake.

'Indeed,' Maeve agreed.

'Yes,' Mrs Oatcake said. 'Message received loud and clear.'

'I might give up the church flowers,' Cathy said, 'and Pete will take over the shopping and cooking.'

Allegra looked at her parents' contented faces and felt delighted. She'd had faith all along they'd sort things out. They were a team.

She suppressed all thoughts of Zack. No point in thinking about him and whether she and he would have ever made a good team. That was all in the past.

Despite what she'd said to Holly in the car, about maybe Zack wanting to send her a message by swapping over the photos, she knew that was unlikely.

He had obviously searched the case when he got it back for her, found the photos and replaced them by mistake with the other set he had.

He must have kept his own photos by chance — Zack wasn't great at sorting out his stuff and tended to hang on to the most unlikely items long after they should have been discarded.

Except me, a voice in her head whispered. He didn't hang on to me.

'May I have a word, Allegra?' Maeve asked. 'In the kitchen?'

'Of course,' Allegra said, surprised.

'This is difficult,' Maeve said, 'but I

feel I owe you an apology. I've owed it to you for a long time and now, to see you sitting there looking so peaky and tired . . .'

'An apology for what?'

'Zack. When you were engaged. I shouldn't have expressed my opinion to you about him.

'I remember saying something rash about him needing to sort out his priorities. I had no right to do so.

'I'm desperately sorry if it had an impact on your relationship. It was unforgivable.'

'Please don't worry, Maeve,' Allegra said. 'I managed to mess up my relationship with Zack all by myself. No-one else's fault.'

'Nevertheless, dear, I feel better for having got that off my chest after all this time. Now, shall we rejoin the others? Oh, here's Mrs Oatcake.'

'Might I have a word, Allegra, dear?' Mrs Oatcake said. 'In private,' she added, looking at Maeve.

'I'll make myself scarce,' Maeve said

with a chuckle. 'You're very popular today!'

'I know we've only just met, but I wanted to tell you, Allegra,' Mrs Oatcake said, 'that when you're young you should be having lots of fun.

'Your father's been telling me he thinks you are married to your violin, but what I have to say is this — I think it would be much more fun to be married to a nice young man. Maybe that Zack your mother's told me about?'

Goodness, Allegra thought. Was there nothing else for people in Bath to think about other than the failed romance between her and Zack?

'You may be right, but . . .'

'Boris!' Holly's cry could be heard.

Allegra rushed through to the hall and found her friend embracing the singer.

'I had to come down,' he said. 'You are all right, aren't you, my darling Holly? I simply couldn't bear it if you weren't.'

'More than all right,' Holly said as she allowed him to envelop her in a comforting hug.

'Ah,' Mrs Oatcake said, as she tottered into the hall. 'See what I mean, my dear? Lots of fun.'

'They're talking about the drama on the radio now!' Pete called from the sitting-room. 'About how they managed to defuse the bomb and avert the danger. It could have been terrible!

'Come in here and listen, everyone.'

'I'm so glad it's all over,' Cathy commented as she budged up on the sofa to accommodate the crowd.

'We owe everything to the bomb squad,' Maeve declared.

'What about the boy who found the bomb?' Cathy reminded her.

'True,' Holly said. 'If he hadn't thought that field looked interesting and asked his brother to take a photo . . .'

'If you hadn't showed me the picture of the nature table,' Mrs Oatcake said to Cathy.

'If you hadn't remembered what a bomb looked like, from the War,' Pete said to Mrs Oatcake.

'A team effort!' Boris decided and

everyone cheered.

Allegra relaxed, stretching her legs out in front of her. She was content and happy to be among friends and family.

There was so much to be grateful for. Life wasn't like a story. Love didn't always work out. Maybe there would be someone for her, one day, but she would have to wait and see.

For now, it was enough to be grateful for what she had, and for the fact they were all safe after a very frightening time.

Reunited

It was nearly Christmas and the weather forecast had mentioned snow.

Allegra squeezed through the crowds at Waterloo Station, anxious to stride out and get some air. She walked quickly over the Golden Jubilee Bridge, taking in the bright skyscrapers with their strange new shapes and the sparkling river below.

She was looking forward to tonight. The opportunity had fallen into her lap of playing a solo at St Martin-in-the-Fields. 'The Lark Ascending', her favourite piece.

She walked past Charing Cross and made her way through the side of Trafalgar Square to St Martin's.

Her parents and other friends coming to the concert would arrive later. She always liked to make her own way to a solo performance, finding it the best solution to coping with her nerves.

Once inside, she went downstairs to her dressing-room and took out her violin, tuning it carefully and running through a few phrases.

As Allegra changed into her concert dress her fluttering nerves turned to excitement and anticipation. She heard other musicians arriving and several members of the orchestra looked in to wish her luck.

'Not that you'll need it — the rehearsal this morning was fabulous.'

★ ★ ★

Now she was climbing the steep steps, making her way up to the side of the stage area. As she walked on, the orchestra was on its feet.

Allegra pulled her bow across the strings to check the tuning. Satisfied, she turned to the conductor and nodded.

She could see her parents in the front row: Cathy with her nails digging into the palm of one hand, as she had done every time she'd watched her daughter play a solo, and Pete with an expression on his face both soppy and proud.

Boris and Holly were here, holding hands — and she could see Cassie and her parents. Maeve and Mrs Oatcake, too. Allegra couldn't believe they'd made the journey up to London to hear her. She was so grateful.

And now Zack was coming in at the back of the church. She could see him, in a dark overcoat, brushing a few flakes of snow from his shoulders.

Except she knew he wasn't there. It was her mind playing tricks.

The orchestra whispered the opening soft, plump chords, like a nest for her lark. First trembling little flurries, then bolder, until up flew the bird, soaring into the roof above.

Allegra closed her eyes. The melodies unfolded and floated through the air, filling the hall.

'The Lark Ascending' had to be one of the most beautiful pieces ever written — a nostalgic reminder of the past; of summer, warmth, tenderness and the countryside.

Allegra thought back to the letter she'd

received from Zack. He wanted her to forgive him for everything.

But how could she, when the mistakes were all hers?

He was at peace over his adoption. He had two families now, and soon, he said, when the time was right, he'd come back to England, to live here again.

He'd told his birth mother all about Allegra and she wanted to meet her. As for the photos, he said it was only when he found them inside the case, after it was sent over from Spain, that he finally realised she must still have feelings for him.

He understood that, if she'd kept them all those years they were apart, safe in her violin case, it must mean he still had a special place in her heart.

The amazing thing was, he'd kept his photos, too. He told her he always carried them around in his wallet, which was why they were as dog-eared as Allegra's. He'd swapped her photos with his photos, hoping she would notice.

Now he carried her photos and she

his. When he came back, if it worked out, it would be a second chance for them. A chance for true love.

Allegra had no idea how long it would take for him to be ready to love her again. But she would be waiting.

The music began to draw to an end, the beautiful fluttering quietening and settling.

* * *

At the end of Allegra's solo, the audience sat poised, then, unable to wait any longer, jumped to their feet.

'Bravo!'

'Encore!'

She was presented with flowers and called back many times by the ecstatic crowd.

Finally, she went back to the dressing-room, the cheering ringing in her ears. She meant to put her violin away and join her parents and friends. But what was this?

The door of the room was ajar and her

242

violin case open. Inside, she saw two sets of photos, hers and Zack's. His grandmother's ruby ring lay alongside.

'Vanessa decided she didn't want it.'

Zack was standing in the doorway.

'Oh, she wants to marry my brother, but both she and Joe wanted me to have the ring back.

'They thought it should be returned so that I could give it to the person I want to spend the rest of my life with.'

Allegra's face lit up and in an instant Zack was by her side.

'You performed beautifully,' he said in a hoarse voice, then kissed her tenderly.

The two of them clung to each other.

'I thought I saw you at the back, but I wasn't sure if I'd imagined it. Zack, I've missed you so much!'

'I can't believe I left you to rush off to America without a proper explanation.'

'You did send me the letter.'

'And you replied.' Zack smiled.

'And our photos are back together, where they belong.'

'Never to be parted. We should frame

them! Hang them over the mantelpiece.'

Allegra nestled happily in Zack's arms.

'Are you back for good?' she asked.

'Yes. I've given my notice in, at the University.

'It was great staying with my mother and her family, but now I want to pick up where I left off, if that's OK?'

'Do you mean . . . ?'

'I love you, darling Allegra. Just answer me one question. Will you marry me?'

'Yes! Yes, Zack. Of course I'll marry you.'

He slipped the ring on to the third finger of her left hand — where, this time, it would stay.

Other titles in the
Linford Romance Library:

TOO LATE FOR LOVE

Wendy Kremer

Kitty will contemplate marrying only for love, and no other reason. No longer a young debutante, she believes she'll be content simply to live with her mother and devote her time to charitable work. Then her acquaintance Lord Wrothem, having decided it is time he found a suitable wife to continue his line, proposes. Unwilling to countenance a marriage of convenience, Kitty rejects him. But she comes to think that she may have been too hasty in making that decision . . .